LONGSHANKS

HE LIFTED HIM CLEAR OF THE GROUND

Longshanks

by

STEPHEN W. MEADER

ILLUSTRATED BY
EDWARD SHENTON

SOUTHERN SKIES

SOUTHERN SKIES
LITTLE ROCK, ARKANSAS
www.southernskies.com

Dedication

*The republication of this book is dedicated with affection
and gratitude to Gil Carrick, whose friendship and
love of music helped to kick start the career of his
friend of 45 years, Jerry Atchley*

ILLUSTRATIONS

CHAPTER I

Down the last long hill into Wheeling Town came
the stage, its four lean horses at a canter and its
brakes squealing under the heavy foot of Long
Bill Mifflin.

The early April sun, which had been promising
Spring all day, was gone now, and a chill rose
with the dusk from the river. The boy on the seat
beside the driver pulled his cloak around him.

''Le's see, now,'' said Long Bill, unwinding the
lash of his sixteen-foot whip. ''Ye say ye hain't
got no friends in the town, here, but I reckon ye
got plenty o' money. So it 'pears like a public
house is the thing. Which one? Well, thar's three
or four good taverns. The one we put up at is the
Gin'ral Jackson. Then thar's the Injun Queen,
an' Burke Howard's place, only I wouldn't coun-
sel ye to go thar. Good licker, good beds, an' bad
company. Most all of 'em will be full now, though,
with the steamboat leavin' tomorrow.''

Tad Hopkins thanked the driver for this information and looked down from his perch with

interest as the big coach lurched through the ruts of Wheeling's main thoroughfare. Soon they came to a stop in the yard of the General Jackson Inn. Tad climbed down, pulled his portmanteau out of the great leather "boot" at the back of the coach, said good-by to his comrade of the past two days, and went into the tavern.

"No beds—not even half a bed," said the inn-keeper with a gesture of finality.

Tad went down the street, jostling his way through crowds of river-men, backwoodsmen, drovers, and traders. Occasionally he passed an elegantly dressed dandy, but for the most part the people he saw were rough and uncouth.

Wheeling, he now realized, was a frontier town of the great West, and he felt a tingle of excite-ment at the thought that he had come to the gate-way of his adventure.

Finding a place to sleep in this alluring outpost seemed a difficult matter, however. The landlord at the Indian Queen was as short in his refusal of lodgings as the first man had been, and at two other taverns where he inquired Tad was met with the same answer. Then, down close to the river-front, he saw a big white-painted frame building with a crude sign that bore the letters "HOTELL."

Lights blazed in the downstairs windows, and a sound of music came from within.

Tad trudged up the steps and entered a large room with a sanded floor. Two fiddlers were scraping away diligently at the farther end of the place, and a crowd of thirty or forty men stood drinking and watching a raggedly dressed old fellow do a buck-and-wing dance.

At one end of the long and busy bar lounged a big, red-haired man in shirt-sleeves. Tad crossed to him.

"Could you put me up for tonight?" he asked.

The man eyed him shrewdly.

"I've got a cot in one of the rooms, but it'll cost ye dear," he answered at length. "Two dollars for the night. An' I doubt ye've that much money."

"Yes," said Tad. "It's high, but I can pay it."

"Let's see your cash," the other replied coldly.

Tad hesitated a second, then pulled a purse from under his belt. The big handful of Government notes and silver which he held up seemed to satisfy the tavern-keeper.

"Two dollars—in advance," he said, with a nod. "That'll cover supper an' breakfast."

Tad paid him and was stuffing the purse back

into its place when he saw a tall, dark man, who had come up during the conversation and was standing a few feet away, leaning an elbow on the bar. He was a rather handsome fellow of twenty-four or twenty-five, with a sweeping, dark mustache and restless, sharp, black eyes. His clothes, beautifully tailored and expensive, seemed to have been worn a little too long or too carelessly. But it was his hands that Tad noticed first of all. They were white and slim, with extraordinarily long fingers. And on the middle finger of the right hand was a queer-shaped silver ring with a dull green stone.

The man shifted his gaze quickly, as Tad looked up, and the next moment he was ordering a drink from one of the bartenders.

"Here, you, Rufus," cried the landlord to a negro boy who emerged just then from the kitchen, "take this feller up to Number Four—lively."

"Yassah, Marse' Burke," was the reply, and Tad, hearing the name, remembered the stage-driver's warning.

"Burke Howard," he thought. "Yes, that was the name. But I've got to sleep somewhere, and at any rate I'll keep my eyes open."

The darky led him upstairs to a large, bare

room with two beds and a small cot. One of the
beds was already occupied by a snoring guest,
and the other had a shabby pair of boots beside
it. Tad left his satchel under the cot and returned to the lower floor. In the great kitchen
just back of the bar he found a long table at one
end of which a few rivermen were noisily finishing
their supper. And sitting down at the other end,
he was soon served with hot beef stew and potatoes. The long, cold ride had made him hungry.
He did full justice to the meal and arose feeling
better. The fiddlers were still playing when he
returned to the main room. He watched awhile,
then took his cloak and went out of the stuffy
atmosphere of the bar into the cool night. A few
steps down the hill brought him to the river front,
and just below was the big gray shape of a steamboat, tied up at the landing. There were a few
lights aboard her, and an occasional rumble of
barrels came from the lower deck where sleepy
stevedores were loading the last of her cargo for
the long voyage down river.

Tad saw a small, lighted office at the landward
end of the dock and picked his way through and
around the scattered piles of freight till he
reached it.

"I want to take passage to New Orleans," he said to the sour-visaged clerk.

The man continued to write an entry in his book, scowling importantly. Then he cast a slow, scornful glance in the boy's direction.

"To New Orleans," he replied, "the fare is forty-five dollars—*forty-five—dollars*—with yer stateroom an' meals, that is. I reckon you mean Cincinnati or maybe Louisville, don't you?"

"No, New Orleans," Tad repeated patiently and drew forth his wallet. "Here's fifty. The name is Thaddeus Hopkins of New York."

Subdued, the clerk gave him his change and his receipt, and Tad climbed the hill once more to Burke Howard's place with a great sense of being a man of the world.

It was not until a half hour later, when he lay in his cot in the big, dark bedroom at the Inn, that his lonesomeness returned.

The man in the farther bed snored steadily with a purring sound, and Tad could not go to sleep, try as he would. Instead he lay there thinking of the events of the last few days and of the journey ahead of him.

It was amazing to realize that less than a week had passed since he received his father's letter. Back at the Academy for Young Gentlemen in southern Pennsylvania, where he had spent the last two winters, it had seemed, five days ago, as if the long routine of lessons would never end. And then, one morning, had come the long envelope from New Orleans, addressed in his father's big, bold hand, and in it had been news!

It was in the breast pocket of his coat now, but he did not need to look at it, for he knew it by heart.

"Dearest Tad," his father had written:

"I hear from Master Lang that you have been doing well in your work. Otherwise I would hesitate to suggest the plan I have in mind. As it is, I believe there can be no harm to your education in leaving the school before the end of the term.

"I shall be sailing for England in a short time, to look after some business, and it has occurred to me that it would make a pleasant vacation for us both if you were to accompany me. There is now a steam-packet leaving Wheeling every fortnight for the South, and I wish you to make ready as soon as possible, so as to sail by the next vessel, on the sixth of April.

"A draft on my bankers is enclosed, which Master Lang will cash for you, and this should provide ample funds for the journey to New Orleans.

"I am looking forward with great joy to our

voyage together, and shall be waiting for you at the levee on the arrival of your steamboat.

"Lovingly, your father,

"JEREMIAH HOPKINS.

"March 12, 1828."

Tad's preparations for departure, watched enviously by the other boys in his form, had filled the next two days. And at daybreak of the third morning he had boarded the Baltimore-to-Wheeling stage.

Crossing the mountains on the great creaking coach, listening to Long Bill Mifflin's stories and watching the road ahead for signs of the deer and bear and mountain lions that the driver assured him filled the woods—all this had made it a journey he would never forget. And now he was in Wheeling with the mighty river running past, not a hundred yards from his bed, and the steampacket *Ohio Belle* waiting to carry him on the long southward slant of nineteen hundred miles to New Orleans.

Tad was genuinely fond of his father, though they had seen little of each other for the past two years. Jeremiah Hopkins was a New York cotton broker of considerable wealth. His interests fre-

quently took him into the South and to Europe,
and after Tad's mother died, he had left the boy
in the care of school-masters.

The prospect of a whole long Spring and Summer spent in voyaging with his father made Tad's
heart thump joyfully. He was just drowsing off,
with rosy thoughts of the future filling his head,
when the door of the room was opened quietly.

A tall figure entered and crossed the room with
slow steps, lurching a little as he walked. There
was no lamp in the place, but a ray of moonlight,
reflected from the wall, lighted the man's face
dimly. As Tad watched, he moved a few paces toward the cot and stood motionless, looking down
at the boy with a somber expression as if he were
deep in thought. Tad looked up from under low-
ered lids, pretending to be asleep, and after a
moment the figure turned away and went over to
the vacant bed. It was the gentleman with the long
white fingers he had seen below in the bar.

For some reason he could not quite define, Tad
was frightened. Surely there was nothing strange
about the man's actions. A little drunk perhaps,
but incidents like that were to be expected in a
river-front tavern. He watched him partially un-
dress and tumble into the bed, where presently his

snores began to mingle with those of the first sleeper. And not till then did Tad draw a full breath.

Stealthily he felt beneath his pillow for the purse. It was there, safe and sound. He wound the leather thong tightly about his fingers and lay quiet, too much disturbed to sleep.

An hour crept by. Somewhere off in the woods back of the town a fox barked, and hound dogs answered with a frenzy of baying. A tipsy roisterer went past, mouthing a river song. Then gradually the noises of the night subsided, and 'Tad dropped off to sleep.

CHAPTER II

Bright April sunshine, streaming in the window
of the room, flooded the bare walls with matter-of-
fact daylight. It shone in Tad's eyes, and he woke
up with a start.

The steamboat! It left at eight. He reached for
his big silver watch under the pillow, and found
to his relief that it was only a few minutes after
six. At the same time he discovered the purse,
still firmly attached to his hand. The terror of
the night seemed ludicrous now. He chuckled at
his own timidity and began dressing rapidly.

The two other occupants of the chamber were
still heavily asleep when Tad doused his face and
hands in the wash basin, strapped his traveling-
bag, and went out.

In the front bar there was only a single cus-
tomer—a humorous-faced little Irishman in brass-
buttoned blue clothes, who sat beside a table with
a glass of hot toddy in one hand and a pipe in the
other.

He looked at Tad jovially. "Bedad, an' it's glad
I am the last barrel is aboard!" he said, quite as
if they had known each other for years.

"Are you one of the steamboat men?" the boy asked.

"I am that, lad—first mate of the *Ohio Belle*, an' a terrible tired one. We've been takin' cargo for two days an' nights on end. An' now I've got a half hour ashore while they're a-gettin' up steam."

"Does she sail in half an hour?" asked Tad.

"Or sooner," replied the Irish mate. "Th' ould man's a driver whin his cargo's once loaded. If it's breakfast ye're thinkin' of, wait and have it aboard with me. I take it ye're bound down river. I've bread and butter and a cold chicken in me locker, and we'll get coffee from that black son o' Ham in the galley. The passengers ain't supposed to begin gettin' their meals aboard till dinner time. But we'll have a breakfast, or my name's not Dennis McCann."

The plan sounded like a good one to Tad. He waited while the mate finished his glass and paid his score; then, shouldering the bulky portmanteau, he followed him down the hill.

"Ye see," said McCann, "this steamboatin' is only a bit of a change like, for me. Me real business is deep-water sailin', as ye may tell by the roll o' me legs."

Already, by twos and threes and singly, people

were going aboard. Tad and his companion shoul-
dered through the crowd that had assembled to
witness the great event of the week, and crossed
the gayly painted gangplank.

Instead of climbing the broad stairway to the
deck above, McCann led the boy forward through
a narrow alleyway just inside the paddle-box
amidships. A blast of heat struck them as they
emerged, and Tad found himself facing a row of
glowing doors, where sweating darkies fed the
boiler-fires with cordwood.

"That's prime, seasoned hickory," shouted the
mate above the roar of the fires. "Don't take long
to get a head o' steam with wood like this. But
wait till ye see the dirty green stuff they give us
down along the lower river."

They went through another passage where the
heat was almost stifling and came out on the forward cargo deck, solidly piled with merchandise.
Climbing a steep, ladder-like companionway, they
reached the main passenger deck. Higher still,
Tad could see the "Texas," or upper deck, with
the pilot house perched atop, and just aft of it
the two tall stacks, with clouds of smoke pouring
from them.

"Rest here awhile, me lad," said McCann,
"whiles I rustle that breakfast."

Tad sat down on his portmanteau, close to the rail, and watched the spectacle below. The passengers made a colorful assemblage. There were plain pioneer folk in linsey-woolsey and butternut cloth, going back to their homesteads in Indiana or Illinois. There were wealthy planters from the cotton States, resplendent in fine raiment and attended by retinues of colored body-servants. Small tradesmen, drovers and the like, from the nearer river towns, made up a fair proportion, and Tad saw two or three lonely-looking hunters in buckskin, with their long rifles and little packs of provisions, bound for the wild western country. One oddly dressed man, with an eyeglass, who was constantly asking questions and jotting down notes in a little book, Tad decided must be an English tourist.

There remained a little group which he found it harder to identify. Three or four men in fashionable frock-coats, their pearl-gray beaver hats cocked at a rakish angle, and clouds of smoke rolling up from their cigars, idled and jested by the landward end of the gangplank. Either they had no luggage, or it was already stowed aboard. Tad did not care for their looks, and he liked them still less when he saw them joined by a companion—the tall, dark fellow whom he had already encountered twice in his brief stay at Wheeling.

The friendly mate returned just then with a steaming pail of coffee and led Tad off to his bunk in the officers' cabin. Breakfast over, McCann rose and put on his mate's cap.

"There goes the 'all ashore' call," said he. "I'll take ye down to the purser, an' ye can get yer room from him."

Tad found the stateroom assigned to him and put his bag inside. It was a tiny cubicle with a single bunk, its window opening on the deck far aft. Outside, the boy joined a group of passengers at the rail.

The last hurried arrivals had rushed aboard, and final preparations for departure were now in progress. Negro deck-hands stood by the mooring ropes at bow and stern. At a signal from the pilot-house the cables were cast off and the darkies burst into song as they hauled them in and coiled them down.

Bells rang sharply in the engine-room. With a creak and a splash the tall paddle-wheels began to turn, and the steamboat, catching the swift current, swept grandly out into the Ohio. A long, bellowing blast of the whistle bade farewell to the waving throngs astern.

That day and those that followed were full of

experiences for Tad. Hour after hour he sat by the rail, or stood on the Texas with his friend the mate, watching the valley unfold. The river was running bank-full, fed by the April freshets; and added to the eight or ten miles an hour of which the steamer was capable, the strong current gave them a speed that seemed almost dizzying.

They shot past dozens of loaded broadhorns and keel-boats, drifting down with a single long steering oar directing their course. The boatmen would cheer the *Ohio Belle* or curse her, depending on their humor and whether or not their craft misbehaved when her wash hit them.

Some of these rude arks held all the worldly possessions of a family—homesteaders setting out to conquer the wilderness in Missouri or Iowa. Many of them had chicken coops on their half-decks, and once Tad saw a yoke of red steers chained to a post amidships and watching the water with rolling, frightened eyes.

He tried to imagine what sort of life the people led, aboard those homely, slow-moving boats. Almost he envied the freckled youngster he saw fishing over the side of one weather-beaten broadhorn. If he weren't going to New Orleans to see his Dad—well, he couldn't help thinking what a lazy, carefree, interesting voyage one could take in an Ohio River flatboat!

To Tad, raised in the more thickly populated country along the Atlantic seaboard, the forest-covered hills that rolled back from the river as far as the eye could see were satisfyingly wild and mysterious. And yet he was surprised at the feeling of bustle and activity that pervaded the valley.

Little settlements of new log houses were continually appearing along the shore, and in many places sheep and cattle were grazing in freshly cleared pastures. Ferry-boats, rowed by lusty river men, plied back and forth between the West Virginia and Ohio villages. Trading scows, loaded with calico, tools, and manufactured goods from the East, put in at the farms and hamlets to exchange their merchandise for produce.

"This is a great country, lad—a great country," Dennis McCann would say. "Some day, belikes, 'twill be almost as great as Ireland!"

Tad watched the pilot spin the huge wheel to left and right, as the *Ohio Belle* splashed her way down through the shallows. There was plenty of water and fairly easy steering, but the skill of the gray-bearded old keel-boat man in the pilot-house seemed uncanny nevertheless. He could sense a sunken snag farther away than Tad could see a floating one. And he seemed to mind steering at night no more than in the daytime.

They stopped at Marietta and later at Parkersburg that first afternoon, and as darkness fell, the chief pilot came up to relieve his assistant, who had had the wheel most of the day. Tad, before he turned in that night, had the thrill of standing in the pilot-house and watching the old-time riverman take his craft down through the inky blackness, swinging the bends like a race horse.

The little stateroom was clean and comfortable in spite of its tiny size, and the boy slept so soundly that not even the hoarse wail of the whistle awoke him.

The *Ohio Belle* made a stop of several hours at Cincinnati to load and unload freight the morning of the third day. And again the following forenoon at Louisville there was a long delay.

The weather, which had been fine up till then, turned cloudy with spits of rain that morning, but Tad, as usual, spent his time on deck with the mate. The river was high enough to make the passage of the Falls a possibility, and the *Ohio Belle,* shallow of draft like all the river steamers, took the white water safely.

The rain increased in the afternoon, and Tad was finally driven inside out of the wet. He had paid very little attention to his fellow passengers on the voyage so far. But now, for something to do, he strolled down the inside passageway to the main saloon. It was just before he reached the cabin companion that he passed a door standing ajar and heard men talking angrily. Suddenly one voice rose to a shout and a chair was pushed back with a violent scraping noise. Then the door opened, and in it, with his back to Tad, stood a tall man in shabby, well-cut clothes. The fellow swayed a little and caught the door-jamb with one hand. With the other he flung a pack of dirty playing-cards back into the room. Then he spoke in a thick, choking voice.

"You've cleaned me," he said. "You've got my last cent, curse you! But I'll be back, and don't you forget it!" As he turned to leave he almost fell over Tad, and the boy was startled by the look of ferocity on his white, drawn face—a face he knew and had begun to fear.

With long strides the man reached the end of the passage, then checked himself in the act of turning the corner, and glanced back at Tad as if he remembered something. An instant later he was gone.

The other gamblers in the stateroom were silent for a moment after his departure. Then one of them burst into a loud guffaw.

"So he'll be back, eh!" he cried. "That's a good 'un. Who'd lend him a plugged nickel on board here?"

They resumed their game, and some one slammed the door shut. Restless, Tad roamed about the interior of the vessel, went down to watch the darkies firing the boilers on the lower deck, watched the Indiana bluffs to the northward slide past in the rain, ate supper with the other cabin passengers, and finally went back to his stateroom. When he had undressed he bolted the door, opened the window a few inches for fresh air, and went to bed. Lulled by the steady beat of the rain, he was soon asleep.

It must have been hours later when he woke, for the downpour had ceased and a gusty wind was blowing. Was it the wind rattling his door that had wakened him? Rubbing his eyes he rose on one elbow and peered over the edge of his bunk. And there, just climbing through the window, was the black, looming figure of a man.

CHAPTER III

For three or four seconds Tad was too terrified to move. Then he recovered his presence of mind and scrambled up, drawing a deep breath to shout for help. But before he could utter a sound the intruder had dropped, cat-like, to the floor of the stateroom and was on him in a bound.

A powerful hand closed on his windpipe, and a gag of some sort was stuffed into his mouth.

Tad, strong and wiry for his fifteen years, fought back at his tall antagonist savagely, but it was an unequal struggle. With a swift skill that argued previous experience, the prowler pulled a cord from under his coat, and twisting the lad over on his stomach, he caught his wrists in a tight hitch behind him. Half a dozen quick passes of the cord, and Tad lay trussed up on the bunk, helpless as a baby.

Then the man rose leisurely, produced a tinder-box from somewhere, and lit a candle, which he stuck on the lid of the box and set down on the floor. Tad, getting a good look at him for the first time, saw that he was masked. A black handkerchief with holes cut in it covered the whole upper part of his face.

With quick fingers the fellow went through Tad's clothes, taking his father's letter, his watch, and a few other trifles, and putting them in his own pocket.

The boy, struggling desperately to get his hands free, had to lie there in anguish and see his treasures taken. At last, as the robber paused, baffled for a moment, Tad felt the knots that held him slip a little. He bent his knees up to loosen the tension between ankles and wrists, and worked his arms cautiously back and forth. One hand slid through, then the other, but he lay still and gave no sign.

The man had opened the portmanteau and was rummaging through it swiftly, but still he did not find what he was after. As he rose, the candle's beam shone full on his right hand and Tad had a momentary glimpse of a ring—silver, with a dull green stone. It was the gambler from Wheeling, who had seen him open his purse to pay for his lodging. Would he give up the search and leave as he had come? It was a foolish hope. At that very instant the fellow turned and stepped over to the bunk, his slim, sure fingers feeling under the pillow where the purse was hidden.

Tad could restrain himself no longer. With a cry, muffled by the gag, he pulled his arms from behind him and leaped upon the thief. Together they went sprawling across the tiny cabin. The candle was kicked over and extinguished and the struggle went on in the dark. Suddenly the gambler shifted his position, and Tad felt an arm tighten about his head with a grip like a vise. His ears began to sing, and all his senses were numbed by the pain of the head-lock. He was powerless to move. Then he became dimly aware that his antagonist was using his other hand to open the door. A draft of cold air struck him and he was pulled out upon the deck. With a suddenness that gave him no time for terror, he felt himself swung up and outward over the rail. And then, as in a bad dream, he was falling—falling.

The shock of the icy water brought him out of his stupor. For a second or two his whole energy was concentrated on getting back to the air again, for the fifteen-foot drop had plunged him deep. As he came up, choking, he pulled the gag out of his mouth and tried once more to call for help. But the stern of the *Ohio Belle* had already gone past, and there was nothing around him but watery blackness.

What should he do now? He was a good swimmer, but the water was almost as cold as in winter, and he knew he could not last long in it. The steamer had been running close to the Indiana shore most of the day, and he had been thrown from the starboard side of the vessel. Something told him to try for the north bank. With the river sweeping down upon him at five or six miles an hour, it was easy to keep his sense of direction. He struck out almost at right angles to the current and swam steadily, saving his strength.

The task seemed endless. As far as he could tell, he might still be miles from land, and he was numb with cold. Twice he had such an attack of shivering that he could not take a stroke for several seconds. His short cotton night-shirt was not much of an impediment to swimming, but the trailing cord was still tied fast to one of his feet, and he used up some of his strength in a vain effort to get rid of it.

Some last reserve of pluck kept his arms and legs going despite the achy weariness that was in them. He thought he saw a blacker mass rising in the blackness ahead, but it seemed to draw no nearer, and he lost hope. Then his toe struck something soft that frightened him. He lashed out desperately to get away from it and struck it again. It was mud. He could stand up, half out of water, and wade. The looming bulk ahead of him must be trees. In another minute or two he was crawling up the bank, so nearly exhausted that he seemed hardly able to move, yet filled·with an indescribable sense of happiness at being alive.

Another attack of shivers made him realize that he must try to get warm. Rising, he half stumbled, half ran along a sort of path that followed the top of the bank. And a moment later, to his joy, he saw a small cabin set in a clearing ahead of him. Hurrying forward, he approached the front of the shack and was about to rouse its inmates by knocking on the door, when two huge dogs came running around the corner and rushed at him. They growled and snapped so viciously at his bare legs that Tad made a hasty retreat, beating them off with the cord which he had removed from his ankle and was still carrying.

"Hello, the house!" he cried.

But the people inside either could not or would not hear him, and after a moment of hesitation a renewed attack by the dogs caused him to keep on his way westward along the bank. The damp twigs and briars slapped and scratched his naked legs, but he was past paying any attention to such trifles. If only he could find a sheltered corner of some sort where he could curl up and rest without perishing of cold!

The path opened after a while on another clearing, bigger than the first, and he made out the shapes of half a dozen scattered houses off to the right, away from the river. There was something depressing in their silent blackness, and after his experience at the last place, he had little heart to approach them. Instead he followed a deeply rutted road that led forward to the bank of what seemed to be a good-sized creek flowing into the Ohio.

Tad groped his way to the door of a log shanty which stood by the water—a store-house of some kind, he thought. But here again he was disappointed, for a heavy padlock secured the latch.

As he stood there, shivering and desperate, his eye fell on a long, dark bulk beside the landing-stage. It was a boat—a clumsy broadhorn of the kind he had seen drifting down the river.

He drew closer and saw a roofed shelter covering the after part. It looked warm and dry. Surely there could be no harm in resting there until daylight. He would come ashore before the owners appeared, he told himself. And a moment later he was scrambling aboard. There were rough, warm burlap bags and a heavy tarpaulin in the shelter. Shivering, he made a place for himself in a deep, snug corner and pulled the canvas cover about him. After a moment or two his body began to warm the nest, and a heavenly peace seemed to soothe his weariness like a drug. Before another minute passed, he had fallen into a slumber far too deep for dreams.

CHAPTER IV

"Hard upon the beach oar—
She moves too slow.
All the way to Shawneetown,
Lo-o-ng time ago-o."

THE SONG came sifting into Tad's consciousness
pleasantly, to the accompaniment of a snapping,
sizzling noise and a most appetizing smell. He
opened his eyes and tried to think where he was,
but everything was dark around him—dark and
strange. He put out a hand and felt bags close by.
Then he remembered in a flash all the details of
the catastrophe that had brought him there. With
a start he sat upright, looking out over the tops
of bales and boxes.

It was not only morning but bright, broad daylight. And the boat was moving. He could see the
line of trees on shore marching past. Painfully,
for he was very stiff and sore, he changed his
position so that he could look out ahead. There in
the waist of the broadhorn, just forward of the
shelter, was a small fire blazing cheerfully on a
rough clay hearth. Over it crouched a young man
in a cap and "store clothes," holding a frying-

pan full of bacon, which gave forth the pleasant aroma he had already noticed.

The tuneful cook resumed his song, adding a verse that took his crew on the next stage of their journey, and Tad, looking beyond him, discovered that there was still another person aboard the flatboat. Up on the half-deck, forward, a big, loose-jointed young fellow of nineteen moved back and forth. In each brown fist he gripped the handle of a fifteen-foot sweep-oar trimmed out of an ash sapling, and pulled steadily and powerfully, walking two steps forward and two back at each stroke. He was dressed in a coarse butternut shirt and fringed leather hunting-breeches, which made a quaint contrast to the more pretentious costume of the man by the fire. He was a tremendously tall youngster—as tall as any one Tad had ever seen—and his gaunt, big-featured, homely face, with the quirk of humor at the corners of his mouth, attracted the boy instantly. He had a mop of tousled, rusty-black hair and deep-set gray eyes that were fixed, at that moment, on the Kentucky shore.

The singer's voice ceased abruptly, and Tad, glancing in his direction, found the man's eyes looking straight into his own.

"Well, I'll be tee-totally—" he began, and

rose, almost dropping the pan. "Looky here, Abe! Leave go them oars an' come a-runnin'."

The young giant in the bows landed amidships in a single long jump.

"What is it? Snakes?" he cried.

For answer the other pointed a finger at Tad, as the boy crawled out of his hiding-place. The look of open-mouthed astonishment on the cook's face had changed now to one of outraged wrath.

"See here, you—you dirty, thievin' skunk!" he blustered. "What in the nation do ye think ye're a-doin' aboard of our—"

His voice was drowned by a roar of good-natured merriment from his tall companion. And Tad, looking down at himself for the first time, realized what a grotesque appearance he presented. The brief night-shirt he had worn when the gambler entered his stateroom had been torn to ribbons in the fight which followed. And after being covered with mud and further ripped by the briars, it was no longer recognizable as a garment. From head to foot he was smeared with dirt and dried blood, and his hair was matted with twigs.

"All right," he grinned, "I don't blame you for laughing, or for thinking I'm a thief, either. But you don't have to worry. I just crawled in here to sleep last night, and—''

''What do ye mean by makin' free with other folks' property?'' began the smaller of the two boatmen. The one called Abe put a restraining hand on his shoulder.

''Shut up, Allen,'' he said. ''Let the boy tell his story. You're cold, ain't you, son? Here, wrap yerself up in this.''

Gratefully, Tad pulled around him the heavy blanket which was offered, and proceeded to give them an outline of his adventure, while Allen continued cooking the breakfast.

''Humph!'' grunted that individual, still sourly, when Tad had finished. ''How much was you robbed of?''

''Not quite two hundred dollars,'' answered the boy.

''Ha, ha!'' chuckled the doubter. ''That's a likely yarn!''

''Wait a minute, Allen,'' Abe interrupted. ''I don't know how much money he had an' don't keer. But I do know when a boy's tellin' the truth. What's your name, sonny?''

''Thaddeus Hopkins,'' answered the boy. ''People generally call me Tad.''

"All right, Tad," the tall young backwoodsman continued. "I reckon the fust thing you're interested in is breakfast. After that we'll see about dressin' you and make some plans.

"Now, Allen, if the viands are prepared you may serve our frugal repast."

There was such a comical dignity in his stiff bow as he made the last remark that both his hearers laughed in spite of themselves. Without more ado they attacked the smoking pile of bacon and cornmeal johnny-cake, and Tad thought no food he had ever eaten had tasted quite so good. There had seemed to be a prodigious lot of it when they started, but the giant sweep-oarsman had an appetite quite in keeping with his huge, gaunt frame, and in fifteen minutes the pans were empty.

"Thar," said Abe as he wiped the last of the bacon grease from his tin plate with a piece of corn bread, "now maybe we can give some attention to navigatin' the good ship *Katy Roby*."

He winked at Tad as he pronounced the name, and Tad, glancing at Allen, saw him flush with embarrassment and turn quickly to the business of cleaning the breakfast utensils.

Abe looked at both banks, to make sure the broadhorn was drifting on the right course, and

rummaged in a pine box under the shelter, astern.
From it he pulled forth presently a pair of woolen
breeches, worn and shrunken, and a clean white
cotton shirt.

"These may fit ye a bit long," he said to Tad,
"but rollin' up the legs an' sleeves won't hurt a
thing. Maybe ye'll grow into 'em."

Tad was really touched, for he could see that
the gangling young boatman had given him his
own "best clothes."

"Thanks," he said. "That's mighty good of
you. And if you don't mind, I'm going to wash
before I put them on."

There was a length of new rope for mooring,
tied to one of the bow-posts, and when Tad had
stripped off his rags he threw the rope over the
side and let himself down into the river. In the
bright morning sun it felt warmer than the night
before, but there was no temptation to stay in
long. He scrubbed off as much of the grime as he
was able, holding on by one hand, and then
clambered back aboard. Five minutes later he was
warm, dry, and decently clad, at least according
to the simple standards of the river.

"Now, Allen," said Abe, resting on his oar-
handles, "what are we a-goin' to do with this
young rooster?"

Allen was frowning in perplexity.

"Got any folks along this part o' the river?"

"No," Tad said. "I don't know a soul between here and New Orleans. But if you want to put me ashore, I suppose I could get something to do and earn my keep until Father comes for me."

Abe shook his head. "That don't seem to me exactly reasonable," he said. "We're a-goin' down to New Orleans ourselves, an' we could maybe use a spare hand. What d'ye say, Cap'n?"

Allen seemed a trifle dubious. "Think the rations'll hold out?" he asked.

"Sartin they will," Abe replied. "We can make it quicker'n we planned, by runnin' nights sometimes. An' with a real dead-shot rifleman like you along, we ought to jest about live on b'ar an' turkey meat, anyhow."

The other member of the crew was somewhat mollified by these words. "Wal, maybe so," said he. "I reckon we can't help ourselves. What can ye do, boy? Cook?"

"I'm sorry," Tad hesitated, "I—I don't think I can, but perhaps I could learn."

"I b'lieve Allen, here, would condescend to give ye a lesson," put in Abe, seriously.

"Hm," said Allen. "Can ye ketch fish, or chop wood?"

"I never tried," answered Tad, "but I'd like to."

Abe, who had been rowing hard during this questioning, leaned on his oars again.

"Now see here," he said, "you don't have to worry about this yere boy. Any youngster with the spunk to wrestle with a robber, an' be dropped off a steamboat into cold water at midnight, an' swim across the Ohio River, an' run three miles, naked, with mean dogs after him—can look out for himself. He'll be cookin, fishin', *an'* choppin' wood long 'fore he gits to New Orleans."

With these words Tad was officially admitted to membership in the crew of the home-made flatboat *Katy Roby* and set forth on one of the strangest and most interesting adventures that ever befell a fifteen-year-old school boy.

All that fine April day they made steady progress down the swollen river. Part of the time Abe and Allen worked at the oars, adding a mile or two an hour to the speed of the current. Part of the time they loafed in the sun on the half-deck, asking Tad questions about the politer world of the Eastern cities and swapping yarns about their own great frontier country.

"You mean to tell me they *all* wear shoes in New York?" asked Abe incredulously.

"Yes," said Tad, "all but a few poor children. I've never gone barefoot since I was a baby."

"Gosh!" the lanky backwoodsman exclaimed. "Look at *my* feet!" He pulled off his moccasin and showed a sole covered by a single vast callus. "Outside of about five months in winter when I wore hide boots, I never had a shoe on my foot till last year. Pap always figgered it was cheaper to let me grow my own leather," he added, with the twinkle in his gray eyes that Tad was learning to expect.

Piecing together what the two boatmen told him and what he picked up from their conversation, he learned that Allen Gentry was the son of a merchant living in the settlement at the mouth of Little Pigeon Creek, where Tad had first sought shelter in the flatboat. His father, James Gentry, was the owner of the craft, and was sending Allen to sell the corn, pork, and potatoes which made up its cargo in the great produce market of New Orleans.

Abe, as he himself told Tad, was merely a "hired hand," sent along to do the heavy work and to "take keer" of Allen. But it was quite apparent that the long-limbed country boy with his quaint humor and his common sense was the real leader of the expedition.

CHAPTER V

WHEN THE LINGERING spring sunset came, the
flatboat was bowling along so merrily that Abe
decided to make a long day's run of it. He left the
bow sweeps and stretched his long bulk on the
little after deck with the steering oar under his
arm. Allen pulled out a home-made banjo from
some mysterious hiding-place and proceeded to
strum it softly. His pleasant tenor voice, floating
out across the reaches of the river, was joined by
a bass bellow from another broadhorn astern, and
for several miles they drifted to the mellow harmony of "Skip to My Lou," "Weevily Wheat,"
"Down the Big River," and "Wabash Gals."

The afterglow dimmed out of the sky, and
bright stars filled it. And Tad, yawning drowsily,
was sent to bed. Rolled up in a blanket on the
hard deck planks and lulled by the murmur of
the river, he slept as soundly as he ever had in
his life.

The sun had already risen when he woke, and
he was surprised to see the budding branches of
a big sycamore overhanging the deck of the flatboat. Abe was up on the bank chopping wood for

the breakfast fire, and Allen was casting off the stern mooring-rope which had been fastened around the tree. Tad threw off his blanket, pulled up a bucket of water from over the side, and hastily performed his morning ablutions.

By the time he had finished, the boat was well on its way again.

"Wal, youngster," chuckled Allen, "how's this? You awake an' ready to eat again?"

The truth was, Tad did have a fine appetite for breakfast, and he admitted it with a grin. "I feel as if I ought to work for it first, though," he said.

"So you can," Abe put in. "Here's the ax. S'pose you split some o' this wood up in nice fine kindlin', while I go up forrard an' persuade her a little with the oars."

Tad, willing enough, picked up the ax and started clumsily to hack away at the chunk of pine. By dint of hard work he managed to split away a cross-grained sliver from one side and was attacking the larger piece again when a smothered choking sound reached his ears. There lay Allen, rolling on the planks and holding his sides with laughter.

In a country where children learned to use an ax almost as soon as they could walk and supplied the house with firewood before they knew their

A-B-C's, the sight of Tad's awkwardness was enough to provoke any man's mirth.

But Abe did not laugh. He left his oars and came down to Tad's side.

"Watch," he said. "You'll git the knack of it in no time." And swinging the ax one-handed, with no apparent effort, he cleft the log cleanly through the center, then into quarters. His arm rose and fell steadily, and in an amazingly short time there was only a neat pile of slender pine splints lying by the hearth.

As they breakfasted, a big keel-boat, piled with farm implements and furniture and with half a dozen lively-looking children swarming over and through everything, steered close to them.

"Movers," said Allen.

A bearded man with a cross, discontented face appeared at the gunwale of the keel-boat and hailed them.

"Where are we? Can you tell me?" he shouted.

"This is the Ohio River," Abe replied cheerfully.

"Yes, but whereabouts—what part?" fretted the mover.

"Jest now," said Abe, considering, "you're in Indianny. But in five more minutes your bow-end'll be in Illinois. Thar's the Wabash, now."

He pointed to the right bank a mile or so below, and Tad saw a wide river emptying into the Ohio from the north.

The bearded man muttered something that might have been thanks and went back to the tiller of the keel-boat, while Abe resumed his breakfast.

"They'll make a mighty valuable addition to the population of whatever place they're a-goin' to," he remarked between mouthfuls of johnny-cake.

"Must be Illinois," put in Allen. "That question sounded jes' like a 'Sucker.'"

The latter scornful epithet, Tad discovered, was universally applied by the Hoosiers to their neighbors on the west. Although hundreds of families were moving from Indiana into Illinois every year and the people of the two States were often blood kin to each other, there was a vigorous rivalry that did not always confine itself to calling names.

Something of this feeling Tad was soon to see, for they made a landing at Shawneetown on the Illinois shore, sometime during the forenoon. One of the first things he had asked his new friends was how he might send word of his safety to his father, in New Orleans. And it had been agreed that they should stop at the first town where steamboats touched and mail a letter.

There were no writing materials aboard the *Katy Roby*. When Abe and Allen had calculations to make, they did it with a burnt stick on the deck planking. So, leaving Allen to guard the flatboat and her cargo, Abe and Tad climbed the muddy hill from the landing-stage and sought a place where paper and ink might be bought. One of the first buildings they reached was a rambling log house with a wide porch in front, which turned out to be a general store. They entered and made their purchases, and Tad started to write his letter, using the head of a barrel for a table. Briefly he described the attempt to put him out of the way and how he had made his escape. Basing his estimate on the average speed of the *Katy Roby,* he wrote that with good luck they would reach New Orleans within two or three weeks.

He was just signing his name to the message when he heard a commotion of some kind outside. The group of loafers who had been hanging around the door when they entered now left the porch with a clatter of boots. A loud voice was raised tauntingly.

"Wal, you long-legged, slab-sided, lousy

Hoosier, want to see how it feels to git thrown?"
it asked.

Tad hastily pocketed his letter and went to the
door. In the midst of a ring of spectators outside,
a big, stocky, river-man was brushing the dirt off
his hands, while a crestfallen youth in torn homespun lifted himself out of the mud.

Abe's long, awkward figure towered above the
group of bystanders. Evidently the champion's
invitation had been addressed to him. He strolled
forward into the ring. "Don't keer 'f I do," he
said.

There were roars of laughter from the Illinois
men.

"Them leather breeches is to scare off the varmints!" one cried.

"What do they feed you on, Longshanks?"
asked another.

"Suckers," answered Abe, with a grin, and
pulled his belt a notch tighter.

The river-man was broad-shouldered and powerful, with short, thick arms like a bear's. He
pounded himself on the chest with a huge fist and
roared:

"Here I am! I'm 'Thick Mike' Milligan o'
Kaskaskia! I kin drink more likker an' walk
straighter, chaw more terbakker an' spit less

juice, break more noses an' swaller less teeth, than any man on the rivers. I eat wildcat fer breakfast an' alligator fer supper. I'm a ragin' hyena! I'm a terror to snakes! Look out, fer I'm a-comin'!''

As he shouted the last words, he jumped in the air and clapped his heels together. Then with a rush he charged at Abe.

There was nothing awkward about the tall Hoosier now. He took a quick sidewise step, springy as a cat on his moccasined feet. One long arm shot out and caught Milligan by his thick neck, spinning him about so that he dropped on one hand and one knee. The river-man was up in an instant, roaring like a bull. But now he came on more warily, trying to get in close, where he could come to grips with his opponent. Abe, circling and retreating constantly, held him out of reach with those long, sinewy scarecrow arms of his.

The onlookers began to hoot and jeer. ''They call that wrastlin' in Indianny?'' yelled one. And another edged close to Abe to trip him.

''Look out!'' cried Tad, but his warning was unnecessary. The lanky young flatboatman had seen the movement out of the corner of his eye, and instead of falling over the outthrust foot he suddenly leaped backward, seized the tricky by-stander by the collar, and hurled him through the air, straight at Milligan. Then, without the loss of a second, he was after the two of them. Catching the river bully off his balance, he lifted him clear of the ground and slammed him on his back, piling the dazed and gasping meddler on top of him before either could collect his wits.

"Thick Mike" picked himself up angrily, while the crowd howled its desire for the "best two out o' three falls!"

Abe seemed to have undergone a change. He was mad now—mad clean through—and his gray eyes blazed as he trod lightly forward to meet Milligan's attack.

The river-man tried a new plan. Waiting till Abe was close, he suddenly plunged in low, hoping to get a crotch-hold and upset the lanky Hoosier. This time Abe wasted no time in dodging. Before the other's hands were fairly on him, he had seized him with both arms around the middle and whirled him, feet in air, over his shoulder. Milligan landed heavily on the small of his back, and with a panther-like spring Abe was on him, pinning his shoulders flat.

There was no longer a question as to which was

the better wrestler, and the stocky Kaskaskia man was the first to admit it. He rose, still a little dizzy from the force of his fall, and shook Abe's hand.

"They ain't many kin do that," he grinned. "How tall air ye, lad?"

"Six foot four," said Abe.

"An' how old?"

"Nineteen," answered the flatboatman.

"Great sufferin' catfish!" the other exclaimed. "Ye'd oughter be a good-sized feller when ye grow up!"

The crowd of loafers did not seem disposed to take their champion's defeat quite so good-humoredly. As Abe and Tad went back to the store to post the letter, these hangers-on followed at their heels.

"Huh! Wrastle? Sure he kin. That ain't nothin'," said one of them. "But what'd he look like in a real ruckus—knock-down an' drag-out?"

The tall youth turned on the top step and deliberately rolled up the sleeves of his shirt.

"Listen," he said, quietly. "One Hoosier to one Sucker ain't a fair fight. But if any two of ye want to tackle me at once, I'll be pleased to accommodate. Step right up here, boys."

His words produced an immediate hush. For a

moment he stood there eyeing them scornfully, while they shuffled their feet and looked sheepish. Then he entered the store.

"Come on, Tad," he said with a wink, "we'll be a-goin' now."

The boy gave his letter to the postmaster, got that worthy's assurance that he would mail it on the steamboat *Nancy Jones*, from Louisville, likely to stop at Shawneetown in the next day or two, and followed Abe down the hill.

Allen, who had heard the shouting, was filled with curiosity. "What'd ye see, boys—a fight?" he asked.

"No," said Abe, "it was jest a demonstration." And chuckling, he went about the business of getting headway on the boat. Allen, however, was not satisfied till he had got a glowing account of the wrestling bout from Tad.

"That's right," he nodded. "This yere Abe is the powerfullest critter ever I see. He kin outrun, outwrastle an' outfight any man in our country, back home—yes, an' outtalk any woman. He's as fast as greased lightnin' and tougher'n a white oak post."

It was early afternoon when they passed the broad mouth of a cave on the Illinois bank. Allen, who had once been as far as Paducah on the steamboat, pointed it out and told the gruesome story of the Wilson Gang, a notorious outlaw band which, twenty-five years earlier, had made the cavern its stronghold.

"Thar was more'n a hundred of 'em," said he, "an' they used to rob boats an' travelers all up an' down the river. They say thar's a sort o' chimney goin' up from that cave into another one over it, an' after the gang was cleaned out, sixty skeletons of murdered folks was found up in that secret cave."

Tad gazed at the place in awe as they drifted past. It looked peaceful enough now. The sun slanted brightly across the gray face of the rock, and a flight of twittering swallows darted in and out of the dusky opening.

They fished and talked, sang and whittled, with alternate spells at the oars, all afternoon, and toward sunset sighted a black cloud of smoke beyond the next bend.

"Steamboat comin'," remarked Abe. A long, mournful whistle-blast came up the river, and they saw a man, at work in a stump-filled clearing, suddenly drop his plow handles and run down to the shore. He leaped in the air, waving his hat frantically as the tall stacks and shining upper works of the craft appeared around the bend.

His horses eyed the approaching monster with
alarm, snorted, reared, and would have dashed
off if the plow had not buried itself and anchored
them.

The steamer passed within a dozen yards of the
flatboat and they read her name, *Amazon,* in
gilded letters across her paddle-boxes. The big
wheels thrashed and churned with a mighty up-
roar as the vessel forced her way up against the
current at all of four or five miles an hour. The
foamy wake that rolled out from her paddle-
wheels caught the *Katy Roby* at an awkward
angle and made her pitch like a steer. Bracing his
feet, Abe pulled on the oars with all his strength
to keep the craft from swinging sidewise. A roar
of laughter went up from the deck of the *Amazon*
where two or three of the crew were gathered.

"Hold her, bean-pole!" shouted one of them.

Abe dropped the oars, picked up a four-foot
stick of firewood, and sent it whirling after the
steamer, already many yards away. He threw so
hard and so true that the billet bounced off the
rail a foot from the fellow's head, and the steamboat men retreated hastily.

Abe grinned as he handled the sweeps again.
"I'm willin' to take their wash," he said, "but not
their sass."

That night, when Allen was tuning up his banjo, Tad went aft to lie by the steering-oar with Abe. He looked at the long, easy frame of the backwoods youth and thought of that morning's wrestling match.

"Jiminy, but you're strong!" he said, admiringly.

Abe shifted his position, looking off at the low stars.

"That's nothin'!" he said gruffly. "I was born big. There's no credit in that. What I'd like is to be able to sing an' play the banjo like Allen. I can't carry a tune any more'n a crow. Or I'd like to go to an academy like you. I bet you've read a power o' books!"

Tad was truthful. "Not such a terrible lot," he said. "They've got a whole library full at school, but when you have to read them, there's no fun in it."

"Gee," murmured Abe, and was silent for a little. Then he turned toward the younger boy, his rugged, homely face serious in the starlight.

"I couldn't git much schoolin', back whar we lived on Little Pigeon," he said. "But I've read some—books like the Life o' Washington, an' the Fourth Reader an' the Bible, an' *Æsop's Fables*, an' the Laws of Indiana, an' *Pilgrim's Progress*, an' *Robinson Crusoe,* an' the Almanac. Guess I've read about all the books I could borrow from any one 'round Gentryville.

" 'Course I learned to write an' cipher in the log school. An' I used to work out the accounts for folks—neighbors—an' write letters for 'em if they had to send news off. I fixed me up a quill pen out of a turkey-buzzard's feather, an' the ink I made out o' blackberry-briar roots an' copperas.

"I'd rather have book-learnin' than all the muscle in the world. They say there's a new University goin' to open in Indiana next Fall. If I was rich, maybe I wouldn't go up thar in a hurry! But I guess I'll likely stay workin' 'round on farms an' boats."

"I should think you'd want to," Tad put in. "If I was as big and husky as you, and could do the things you can, I'd never go back to school."

"Thar," chuckled Abe, "you've put your finger on it. I seem to be a born corn-husker. An' that's all right, too. I like an ax. I like to work with an ax, splittin' rails, buildin' things. An' I like to plow, an' hoe, an' take care o' cattle. Only," he paused, frowning, "some way, that ain't enough." And for many minutes thereafter he sat buried in thought, his chin in his hand. Tad, respecting the stern, almost sad expression on the older boy's face, rose quietly and joined Allen up forward.

Allen finished his song and greeted him. "What's the matter—Abe got one of his silent spells?" he asked. "Don't mind him. He's all right—jes' shiftless an' dreamy sometimes."

And striking a chord or two, he launched into the stanzas of "Old Aunt Phoebe."

CHAPTER VI

They were peeling potatoes for the noon meal on the fourth day of the flatboat's voyage when Tad chanced to look off to the southward and stood up suddenly, with an exclamation of wonder. Above the Kentucky bluffs a cloud was rising swiftly—a living cloud of beating wings.

"Pigeons!" said Abe. And Allen, springing to his feet, ran back under the shelter to get his fowling-piece.

The great flight of birds came swiftly. Before Allen could finish loading the long-barreled shotgun, the first of them were winging over—twos and threes and fifties, and then thousands—so many that they seemed to cover the sky. A vast, vibrating hum of wings filled the air.

Allen rammed home his charge and lifted the gun. Taking aim was hardly necessary. He pointed where the flock seemed thickest and fired. At the loud report a sort of eddying movement went through the nearer part of the cloud of birds, but there was no change in the speed or direction of the flight.

Then bodies of dead and wounded pigeons began dropping like feathered hailstones into the river. They sent up little splashes of water. There must have been a dozen at least.

Only one pigeon fell aboard the *Katy Roby*. Tad picked up the warm, plump body and held it, watching the eyes glaze. The sleek brownish-gray feathers were ruffled, and a shot had carried away part of the long tail.

Allen was grumbling. "One pigeon! I hit plenty, but they all fell in the water. We'd oughter have a dog along to fetch 'em." He was reloading rapidly while he talked, and raised the gun again, looking for the likeliest place to shoot.

Abe's voice came from the bows.

"Don't kill any more of 'em, Allen," he said with something like a command in his tone. "Spose'n you *should* git one or two more to fall in the boat. It takes more'n three pigeons to make a meal for this crew. You ain't jest shootin' 'em for the fun of it, are you?"

"Well, why not?" replied young Gentry with a scowl. "Thar's millions an' millions. Look at 'em!" He waved his arm in a wide arc. "They're so thick they're 'most a nuisance."

"No, sir," Abe answered. "They never harm crops, do they? An' they're pretty, an' hev a right to live. They're bein' killed off too fast as it is. My Pap says when he was a boy in Kaintuck' there used to be four or five flights every year when the pigeons would make the sun dark for a whole day. You don't see that now. This flock here is 'most over now. That's what comes o' killin' 'em by the bushel jest for the sport of it.''

Even as he spoke, the rear guard of the flock swept over, leaving the sky clear once more. The dark cloud of beating wings drew away rapidly to the north, and in a moment the only traces of the event were the stiffening body in Tad's hand and the acrid smell of burnt powder as Allen sulkily set about cleaning his gun.

When dinner was over, the long-legged back-woods boy rose, stretched and climbed to the for-ward deck. Before picking up the oars he shaded his eyes with his hand and looked away south-westward.

"Boys," he said, "unless I'm mighty mistook, we'll pass Cairo an' be sailin' down the Mississippi before night."

"Huh," snorted Allen, "what do *you* know 'bout it? This ain't the headwaters o' Little Pigeon Creek ye're a-navigatin'!"

"Reckon I'm as wise an ol' barnacle as any aboard this packet," Abe replied with a twinkle. "Whar do *you* figger us to be, Cap'n Gentry?"

"Wal, le's see, now," said Allen. "We sighted Paducah jes' before noon. Now I fergit how many miles it is from thar, but seems like they told me it was a full day's run, that time I was down thar I told ye about."

The argument went on spasmodically for the balance of the afternoon. But Abe, as usual, was right.

An hour after sunset, in the calm blue dusk, they floated out of the Ohio with the broad current of the Mississippi sweeping down in a resistless muddy tide from the northwest. They knew the power of that flood a moment later when another broadhorn, just below them, was caught in an eddy and whirled end for end like a twig in a brook.

Abe pulled with might and main on the starboard oar, and Allen swung the steering sweep to bring them over toward the Kentucky shore. "We might's well stay this side whar it ain't so yaller, long as we kin," said the big bow-oarsman. "I feel sort o' more at home in water that might ha' come down from Little Pigeon."

They tied up to the Kentucky bank while it was still light enough to find a good mooring-place. Not much singing or hilarity aboard that night. Something of the vast, brooding mystery of the river had got into them. Tad didn't feel afraid, or even lonesome, exactly. He just wasn't in a mood for talking. The immense distances, the wildness of the country, the hurrying, watery sounds of the mile-wide flood—perhaps it was none of these, or all of them combined, that weighed down their spirits.

"Spooky, ain't it?" said Allen, shaking himself uneasily, and he went to his blankets without taking out the banjo.

Tad followed soon and left Abe sitting hunched in dark silhouette against the stars, his big hands gripped around his knees and his eyes on the shadowy line of willows and cottonwoods across the river. He was used to spells of sadness. This one seemed no worse than usual.

Morning made a difference. The sun shone on budding leaves of tender green and sparkled on the dimpling surface of the water. A perfect riot of bird-song filled the air. In the big trees that overhung the mooring place there must have been hundreds of warblers, finches and song-sparrows, and several times Tad caught the red flash of a cardinal among the branches.

Allen sang and Tad whistled intermittently while they cooked and ate breakfast, and even Abe hummed something that might have been

"Turkey in the Straw" and danced a home-made double shuffle on the foredeck, as he cast off.

"Make the most of it, boys," he laughed. "This is all the Spring we're a-goin' to see. By day after tomorrer we'll ketch up with Summer, at this rate."

The sun was warm enough that day to give truth to the tall boy's words. They passed islands where the dogwood, at the height of its bloom, made a white canopy almost to the water's edge. And in fields along the shore there were bare-footed children running about in calico frocks.

The river did not seem lonesome in daylight. Above and below them they could see busy specks that were keel-boats and barges. They overtook one of these toward noon—a shabby old trading-scow. On its after part was built a little house, or "caboose," from which a length of rusty stove-pipe projected. And a dingy bit of what had once been bright cotton print waved in tatters at the top of a pole. Despite the forlorn appearance of the craft, cheerful sounds came from it, as the Indiana flatboat drew alongside.

A squat, broad-shouldered old man with a bushy gray beard and merry eyes was sitting on a box, forward of the caboose, scraping away lustily at a backwoods fiddle, and thumping time with one foot on the deck. And sitting facing him, apparently entranced by the hoarse squeaking of the fiddle, was a fine red setter dog.

The old fellow finished his tune with a flourish and swung about on his box.

"Howdy, boys!" he cried. "I'm Moses Magoon o' the Big Sandy, peaceful trader an' musician by choice, but a bad 'un when raised. Mebbe you've heard o' these half-horse, half-alligator fellers. I'm one-third horse, one-third alligator, an' the other third mixed catamount an' copperhead. What d'ye find yerselves in need of today? I've got calico, buttons an' sewin' thread, extra fine pantaloons, shoe leather an' wheaten flour, pots an' pans, powder an' lead, candles, salt, nutmegs, an' red pepper."

All this had been said in a loud, hearty voice and without any apparent pause for breath. Mr. Magoon was about to continue when Abe interrupted by laying an oar across the bow of the trading-boat and pulling the two craft together, side by side. This maneuver was not to the liking of the setter, which jumped up, growling, teeth bared for action.

"Be still, Fanny," said the old man quietly. With a dexterous motion he pulled an old-fashioned horse pistol out of the box beneath him and laid it across his knees. At the sight of this weapon, fully eighteen inches long, Abe's jaw dropped comically.

"Hol' on!" he exclaimed, and hastily withdrew the foot he was about to set aboard the scow. " 'Pears like we'd better introduce *our*selves, too. We're the law-abidin'est, softest-spoke flatboat crew betwixt this an' the Falls o' the Ohio. We're two-thirds fishin' worm an' three-quarters turtle-dove. All we want's a chance to trade some good salt pork an' 'taters fer a pair o' them extra fine pantaloons—boy size—'bout big enough fer young Tad here. Ef you'll jes' put away that blunderbuss an' explain the purpose of our visit to Miss Fanny, we'll come aboard an' do business."

Magoon's whiskers parted to display a set of strong, even teeth. He tipped his head back and roared with laughter. "So ye shall," he said at last, and wiped the tears from his eyes with the back of a weather-browned hand. "Durned ef I ever heerd sech a brag as that on any o' the rivers," he chuckled. "But I'll guar'ntee the fishin' worms an' turtle-doves kin take keer o' theirselves when they hafter."

He rose, thrust the pistol back into its hiding-place, and limped over to the gunwale with outstretched hand. "Make yerselves to home," he said.

They lashed the two boats loosely with a length of rope, and Allen stayed aboard the *Katy Roby* to steer, while Abe and Tad made their purchase. They picked out a pair of serviceable brown home-spun breeches from the merchant's stock, and for them traded two flitches of bacon and a barrel of apples.

Allen, with an eye to the profit of the voyage, started to raise some objection, but Abe merely answered, "I'll pay fer 'em when I git my wages," and went on rolling out the barrel.

When the transaction was completed, the genial trader looked up at the sun and whistled. "What about dinner?" he asked. "I've got a big cat-fish here—more'n Fanny an' me could eat in a week. S'pose I make some hot coals an' we'll broil him on a plank."

The Hoosier crew were in hearty agreement with this idea, and while Abe relieved him at the steering-oar, Allen set about making corn-bread as their share of the feast.

Tad, who had no special chores to perform, stayed aboard the scow and got better acquainted with Magoon and the red setter.

The old river-man had an ingenious sort of

Dutch oven built into the wall of the caboose. Adding dry wood to his fire, he soon had a brisk blaze roaring up the chimney. Meanwhile he proceeded to clean and split the catfish, and peg it out on a piece of plank which had evidently been used before for the purpose.

"That pistol," said Moses Magoon, "my ol' Pap toted over the mountings from North Caroliny in 'seventy-nine. It's old an' rusty an' ain't been fired fer fifteen year. 'Tain't even loaded now, but I keep it handy to persuade some o' these thievin' river toughs with.

"I been cruisin' up an' down the Mississip' an' the Ohio ever since I was a young feller, an' I've run afoul of 'em all, one time or another. Jes' last week here, a big keel-boat with half a dozen men on deck come up alongside, somethin' like you did. It was Little Billy, an' his gang, from up the North Fork o' Muddy Run, an' I figgered I was in fer trouble.

"But this yere Little Billy has only got his eye out fer two things—money an' whisky—an' I don't carry neither one of 'em. I let him come aboard an' look, an' he never laid hand on any o' my goods—jes' as polite as you please. 'Well,' says he, 'long as ye ain't got no Kaintucky redeye, what'll ye take fer the dog?'

" 'Sorry, Mister,' I says, an' I was scairt. 'She ain't no ways fer sale,' I says. 'She'd break her heart an' die if I let her go.' An' Little Billy, he jes' grins an' says, 'Right, I had a good dog myself, once.' An' with that he steps back on his keel-boat an' off they go.

"I had a bad time, couple o' years back, with Mike Fink—him they call 'The Snag,' " the old trader went on. "I landed at New Madrid one night an' went up to the store. When I come back, with my arms full o' provisions, I see another boat tied up, close above. An' jest as I was goin' to step aboard mine, eight or ten men that had been layin' low under the bank stood up thar in the dark. One of 'em says, 'All right, stranger, we'll take keer o' this,' an' he grabs the provisions. Then they march me aboard o' my own craft an' tell me to show 'em whar my money is an' no monkey business. I acted like I was plumb scairt to death—teeth a-chatterin' an' knees a-shakin'.

" 'All right,' I finally whispers, 'I'll show ye whar it's hid, only thar ain't room fer but two to go in.'

"Mike Fink swings 'round to his gang. 'Git back on shore, ye lousy varmints!' he bellers. When they're all up on the bank, he pulls out his

knife an' holds it in his teeth, an' I lead the way
into the caboose here. It's a right dark night an'
Mike he strikes a light an' holds up a candle,
while I'm rummagin' round in the corner. Pretty
soon I undo the ketch o' this leetle trap door down
here in the bulkhead, an' open her up. 'Whar's
that go?' says the Snag. 'That's my secret hidin-
place,' I says—'want me to go first, or you?' An'
I'm still lettin' on to be tremblin' so I kin hardly
talk.

" 'You,' says Mike, 'an' by the ol' 'Tarnation
I'll cut you into stewin' meat if you try any
tricks.'

"So I crawls through the hole on my hands an
knees, an' waits fer him to follow."

Magoon opened the little trap door as he spoke,
and Tad laughed when he saw a two-foot ledge of
deck and then the river beyond it.

"Wal," the old man went on, "Mike didn't
come through, right off, an' I tell you I *was*
scairt. 'Twas so durn dark outside, I knew he
couldn't see, but he stayed thar an' tried to figger
if I was up to anything. Finally he says, 'Bring
the money out here in the cabin.' I'm workin' at
the moorin'-rope all this time, an' now I make a
noise like I'm tuggin' an' liftin'. 'Can't,' says I.
'It's too heavy!'

"That fetched him, sure 'nough. Here he comes on all fours, with the knife still in his teeth. I gives the rope one last pull an' it comes away, an' then 'fore he rightly sees whar he is, I ketches him by the scruff o' the neck an' heaves him overboard.

"You can bet I didn't wait to see whether he was drowned, neither. I give a big shove with the oar an' got out o' reach o' the bank, an' then I stood by the gunwale with an ax, ready to cut the hands off anybody that tried to swim out an' climb aboard.

"It must have took Mike a few minutes to crawl out an' git organized again. Anyhow they never follered me."

The last part of the story had been told out on the open deck, and Abe and Allen were listening with rapt attention.

"Is that the same Mike Fink they call the 'Snappin' Turtle' up our way?" asked Abe.

"That's him," the old man nodded. "He's called that above the Wabash. Both names is too good fer him. Wal, boys, how's the dinner comin' along?"

Tad's mind was filled with questions about the river pirates, but he postponed asking them long

enough to do full justice to the planked catfish.
When the meal was over he perched himself on
the gunwale of the trading-boat and waited for
the grizzled river-man to get his cob pipe going.

"Mr. Magoon," he said, when the blue smoke-
clouds were rising at last, "who do you think is
the worst outlaw you ever ran across?"

The old man puffed in silence for a moment.
"Reckon the worst I ever see with my personal
eyes was ol' Jericho Wilson o' the Cave Gang,"
he replied at length. "Him an' Black Carnahan
an' Earless Jake Rogers was a bad bunch. They
had more'n a hundred men to back 'em up, an'
kep' the whole Ohio Valley scairt fer a while.
When that posse of up-river hunters wiped 'em
out, I know mighty well we all breathed easier.

"But listen to me, boy. Fer real cold-blooded,
cutthroat deviltry, nobody on any o' the rivers
kin touch this man John Murrell. He an' his gang
hang out on an island somewhere down beyond
Natchez. He started as a gambler, hoss-thief, an'
murderer, but his main trade nowadays is stealin'
niggers. They say he's killed twenty-eight men
himself, an' gosh knows how many the rest o' the
gang have put away. Mostly he works along the
lower river, but once in a while, when things git

too hot around the plantations, he stays out o'
sight fer a while, mebbe up the Ohio, or over in
Alabama.''

''Did you ever see him?'' asked Tad.

''Not me, an' I hope the day don't soon come!''
said Magoon, fervently. ''They tell me he's a tall,
pale-faced sort o' feller, with dead black hair like
a Frenchman. But the chances are you'll never
run afoul of him. He don't bother with flatboats
much. He's out for bigger game.''

He got up from his box and looked over at the
eastern shore, shading his eyes with his hand.
Some one on the bank was waving a white cloth
to and fro.

''That's a signal fer me to land,'' he said.
''The folks along the river know a tradin'-scow
by the calico flag, an' wave to us when they want
us.''

Tad got back aboard the *Katy Roby,* and they
cast off the tie-rope.

''Wal, so long, Hoosiers,'' said Magoon.
''Reckon I won't see ye again, less'n I ketch ye
in New Orleans. Take keer o' yerselves. Ho, ho!
Fishin' worms an' suckin' doves! Heh, heh!''
And he was still chuckling over Abe's words and
repeating them to Fanny, the setter, as the two
boats drifted apart.

Tad watched the odd little craft until its owner was no longer visible in the distance. Then he looked down at the coarse, homely pantaloons that covered his legs. In spite of himself he could not help a little smile as he thought of the spectacle he would present to one of his carefully attired schoolmates.

Abe saw the smile, and his face lit with pleasure.

"Like 'em, Tad?" he asked.

"You bet," said Tad stoutly. "But listen, Abe, you oughtn't to do this for me. How much does Mr. Gentry pay you, anyway?"

"That's all right," replied the big backwoodsman, grinning proudly. "I git eight dollars a month an' my steamboat passage home."

And with that he vaulted to the fore deck and picked up the oars.

CHAPTER VII

THE CURRENT set over strongly toward the Kentucky shore that afternoon, and soon they found themselves swinging around the outer side of an immense bend. At noon they had been heading almost due south. By three o'clock they were running northwest, and an hour later they were carried over to the Missouri side as another great sweep began, this time to the left.

"That must be New Madrid," said Allen. "The river makes a big S, an' the town lays right in the second bend."

They saw a settlement of twenty or thirty houses sprawled along the bank, with a white church rising from trees above the landing. The river ran fast around the bend, and Abe had left the oars to man the steering-sweep. "Want to land?" he shouted. "Guess we don't need nothin'," said Allen. "After hearin' what happened to that trader feller at New Madrid I'd jest as leave sleep farther down."

They shot past the drowsy town and swung southward again with the hurrying brown flood.

Instead of the wilderness of willow-clad banks and reedy marshes past which they had been drifting, the Missouri shore stretched away here in broad acres of plowed ground.

At sunset they saw ahead of them a big, white-painted house set among trees on a knoll. A broad, rolling lawn stretched down from it to the river, and there were barns and outbuildings half hidden by shrubbery at the rear. Beyond the expanse of lawn and nearer the river, was a less pretentious house, flanked by a row of trim cabins. There were a dozen or more of these, each with its small garden and a curl of blue smoke coming from the chimney.

"Golly," said Abe, "ain't that a pretty layout? S'pose we could git some good clear water here? I'm all clogged up with yaller mud, drinkin' this river water. Let's land anyhow."

He steered inshore and tossed a snubbing-rope over one of the piles at the end of the little landing. When they had made the *Katy Roby* fast, Abe and Allen went up the path toward the smaller house at the end of the line of cabins.

A big man in riding-boots and a wide-brimmed black hat was sitting on the veranda. He had a long, drooping mustache from which a black cigar protruded at a ferocious angle. Altogether he did not look particularly hospitable. Abe stood awkwardly at the foot of the steps.

"Evenin'," said he. "I reckon a place as fine an' handsome as this must have a good well o' water. Ef it ain't too much trouble, we'd like to fill up a kaig or two."

The man got up and took the cigar from his mouth. Under the huge mustache he smiled, and his whole expression grew more friendly.

"No trouble whatsomever, stranger," he answered. "We have to watch out down yere on account o' these river scalawags that steals our shoats an' chickens. But now I know ye ain't that breed o' varmints, fo' they won't drink nothin' but straight Mississip' water, one-third mud an' two-thirds liquid. Bring yo bar'l right along up, an' make yo'selves free o' the landin', ef yo're stayin' all night."

They rolled their big water-keg up to the plantation well, where a couple of grinning darkies filled it for them.

As they came back past the row of slave shanties, a pleasant smell of bacon and corn-pone drifted out to their nostrils. Half a dozen negroes —strapping black field-hands in cotton shirts and trousers—lounged on the grass in front of the cabins. One drew weird minor chords from a home-made banjo, and the others were "patting Juba" as they swayed and sang.

Rolling bass and rich husky tenor blended in a throbbing harmony that sent shivers of delight up and down Tad's spine. It was the first time he had ever heard negroes singing a plantation song. After they had reached the landing and were getting supper aboard the flatboat, the words still came drifting down to them:

"Oh, I long fo' to reach dat heavenly sho',
    To meet ol' Peter standin' at de do';
He say to me, 'Oh, how you do?
    Come set right yonner in de golden pew.' "

"Gosh," said Abe, "those boys shore can sing."

Allen nodded. "Ye'd oughter hear 'em when they git really worked up to it," said he. "That time I was down to Paducah, there was a big gang of 'em aboard the steamboat, bein' took down to New Orleans. Sing! Boy, you'd thought they was goin' on a picnic!"

"Pore things," said Abe.

"Aw, shucks," Allen laughed. "Thar goes your tender-heartedness again, Abe. 'Tain't no use feelin' sorry fer 'em, no more than cattle goin' to market."

Abe shook his head, thoughtfully. "It's not

exactly the same,'' he said. ''They *ain't* cattle, no matter how much folks say so. You take it on a plantation like this one an' they look to be well kept an' happy enough. But s'pose this owner dies, or gits a new overseer. Right off, mebbe inside a week's time, they're bein' starved, or whipped, or sold down the river—families broke up—everything changed.

''Misery comes to white folks, too, but at least they've got somethin' to say about it. Looks like we have to have the slaves to raise cotton. But we ought to make it more of a square deal.''

''Oh, well,'' yawned Allen, ''what's the use of arguin'? 'Tain't likely any of us'll ever be bothered about it, one way or t'other.''

They followed the overseer's suggestion and spent that night tied up at the plantation landing. The last thing Tad heard before he dropped off to sleep was a broken strain of that barbaric music —a low, sobbing croon, inexpressibly sad—borne down on the night wind from the slave quarters.

The crew of the *Katy Roby* were up betimes next morning.

''We're runnin' slow,'' said Abe. ''Got to do some rowin' or we won't be in New Orleans on schedule. Come on thar, cooks an' cook's helpers, git that fry-pan hot!'' And he bent his long back to the oars with a vigor that made the ash wood creak.

Within an hour they had left civilization behind them again and were slipping down through the wildest-looking country they had yet encountered. There were many islands, some hardly more than sand-bars where the twisting, gnawing river was depositing the tons of yellow mud it had eaten away, farther up. Jungles of tall cane lined the banks, and often, when the current bore them through a narrow cut, they would pass so close that the cane rattled along the side of the boat.

They were just entering one of these channels, sometime in the middle of the afternoon, and Allen and Tad were speculating as to whether they were yet in Tennessee, when Abe held up his hand for silence.

"Listen," he said, after a moment. "Dogs barkin', down in the canebrake. Mebbe we'll see what they're a-huntin'."

The others climbed to the fore deck and stood quiet, listening. Soon they too heard the savage baying of the hounds, away to the south, and as the current brought them nearer they watched the banks intently.

The sound was much closer now, and seemed to have changed in tone. There were short breathless barks and an undercurrent of fierce snarling.

"They've got somethin', sure!" said Abe. "An' if they ain't too far back from the river we'll come in sight of 'em in a minute."

"Look!" cried Tad.

As he pointed they saw a gaunt black bear, with two cubs running at her side, dash across an opening in the canebrake not twenty yards away.

Close on their heels came the dogs—big mongrel hounds that leaped abreast of the hindmost cub and pulled him down with murderous jaws. The old bear had started into the cane on the far side of the opening but turned at a scream from her luckless baby. With a rumbling growl she rushed back into the tangle of dogs, knocking them to right and left with vicious blows of her great forepaws.

The other cub had taken to the water and was swimming strongly out across the channel.

"Back water with the oars!" shouted Abe from the stern. And lifting the long sweep from its chocks, he thrust it down into the mud like a setting-pole. The flatboat slackened speed and came to a stop. Leaning far out over the gunwale and stretching his long arm downward, Abe gripped the young bear by the scruff of the neck and hauled him aboard, dripping and gasping.

Meanwhile events had developed swiftly on the shore. There was a noise of running feet, and a hunter in deerskin burst out of the cane. As he appeared, the mother bear left her dead cub and plunged into the river. The next second the man came bounding after her, with no weapon but the long hunting-knife he gripped in his right hand.

The bear saw the flatboat, hesitated, and doubled back to the left, only to meet the hunter, who sprang to bar her last path of escape. With a grunt of rage the great black beast surged up on her hind feet and faced this enemy, standing chest-deep in the water before her.

There was something deadly about the slow advance of the bear, her head sunk between hulking shoulders, and her lips curled back savagely over her great, keen eye-teeth. Cool and tense, the man pulled off his coonskin cap with his left hand. And at the moment when the bear lunged toward him, he waved the furry headgear, with its big, flapping tail, almost in her face. There was a great splash of water as the enraged brute struck downward at the moving object. And so swiftly that the boys' eyes could scarcely follow it, the hunter's foot-long blade was driven home behind her left shoulder. A vivid spurt of crimson tinged the water, and the huge animal made for the shore with a convulsive bound that swept her adversary off his feet. He was up the next instant, shaking the water out of his hair, and with the knife held ready, he followed his victim up the bank. There was no need for another blow. Halfway out of the water, the bear had coughed and stumbled, and when he reached her there was only a limp furry bulk at the edge of the cane.

The crew of the flatboat had watched this encounter, speechless except for a shout or two of encouragement. Now, as the victor drove off the dogs and stooped to examine the slain cub, Allen looked around with a grin of admiration.

"Phew!" he breathed. "No wonder they call 'em half a horse an' half an alligator. Chase a b'ar 'cross country, ketch up with her, an' kill her with a knife in four foot o' water! Glory be!"

The man wrung some of the water out of his fringed buckskin shirt, then turned toward the *Katy Roby*. Abe was still holding the boat against the current, bracing his weight on the long steering-sweep. It was to him that the hunter now addressed himself.

"Wal, stranger," he said, "who does that-air cub belong to—you or me?" He spoke without heat, in a clear, drawling voice that had a steely ring in its undertone.

Abe was silent, looking back at him appraisingly. The man was big-framed, powerfully muscled, lean as a stag. He had straight black hair, worn long, after the fashion of the Tennessee hunters. His strong, fearless face with its big hooked nose looked like an Indian's.

"Ye see, b'ar scalps is wu'th a dollar apiece in Nashville," the hunter proceeded. "The old un's skin'll bring mebbe four dollars more, but I've been trackin' these three fer nigh a week. That's how I make my livin', mostly."

Abe looked down at the cub, which squatted between Tad's knees, licking its fur dry with a long pink tongue.

" 'Pears like the leetle feller got away, fair an' square," he replied. "He'd have made the other bank if we hadn't been thar to pick him up. An' I reckon the boy here would like to keep him. Tell ye what I'll do. I'll wrastle ye fer him."

The man on the bank shot a keen glance at Abe. "Huh!" said he. "Good 'nough. Quick as I kin git this job done, we'll slip on down to the next cleared spot an' see 'bout it."

With that he stooped and deftly cut a circle around the head of the dead cub, lifting off its scalp with the ears attached. Then he set to work on the big bear and in an incredibly short space of time, he had stripped off the heavy pelt and rolled it up, hair inside. From the haunches he cut some chunks of meat which he pierced with a sharp stick and swung over his shoulder. And whistling to the hounds, he picked up his rifle and powder-horn and set out along the bank.

Abe kept the boat within sight of him except when the high cane occasionally swallowed him up. The lanky Indiana boy had little to say as he worked the boat slowly down-channel.

"What about it, Abe?" chattered Allen. "Think ye kin throw him? He looks powerful stout to me. Don't you count on keepin' that b'ar too durn much, Tad."

But Tad, looking up into the weather-tanned countenance of the steersman, saw a twinkle, deep in the gray eyes, that reassured him.

"Why," said he to Allen, "you told me yourself he could throw anybody on the river."

"On Little Pigeon, that was," Allen amended. "I didn't say nothin' 'bout the Mississippi."

Below them a sandy point thrust out from the Tennessee bank, where the river was making land faster than the rank growth could cover it. There the hunter paused and waved to them to come ashore. They tied the flatboat to a stump a little way above, where there was water enough to land,

and strolled down to the sand-bar. Tad led the cub by a piece of rope knotted about its neck.

The stranger was already stripping for action. He pulled off his leather hunting-frock and his inside shirt of wool and stood forth naked to the waist, his big, muscular arms and mighty chest gleaming in the sun. Abe made similar preparations. To Tad's joy, the long-limbed Hoosier appeared no less impressive than his rival. There was a look of whalebone toughness in the tall lad's physique that made up for any difference in bulk.

As they faced each other, the hunter seemed to swell, visibly, like a ruffling rooster.

"Whoopee!" he crowed. "I'm the high-an'-mighty boss b'ar-killer o' the Tennessee bottoms. When I open my mouth all the big b'ars an' little b'ars fer a hundred mile up an' down the river start skedaddlin'. I'd ruther wrastle than eat, an' I give ye warnin', I'm gwine ter git that cub, or my name ain't Davy Crockett!"

He accompanied all this with a droll flapping of the arms, and as he shouted the last words he launched himself through the air at his young adversary.

CHAPTER VIII

THAT WAS a wrestling-match that Tad never forgot. Abe met the opening rush of the Tennesseean with an old trick, but a good one. Crouching just at the right time, he caught the hunter around the knees and lifted him, letting the momentum of his charge carry him on over Abe's shoulder. Instantly the young Hoosier spun about and gripped his rival's body almost before it touched the ground. But Crockett broke the hold with a great writhing twist and rolled over to light on his feet like a fighting cat.

After that they came together more cautiously, each seeming to realize that he was dealing with an opponent beyond the common run. They stepped in and out with a swift padding of moccasined feet, their hands sparring for grips. Twice they went down together, with Abe underneath, for he was finding his antagonist tremendously fast and strong. But the lanky flatboatman could turn quickly, too, and he refused to stay under long enough to have his shoulders pinned to the sand.

Minutes went by, and still the two kept up their

furious pace. It was hot in the sun. Sweat streamed from their bodies, and they panted hoarsely each time they came to grips. But there was no easing off in the ferocity of their attack.

To Tad, watching breathlessly and shouting encouragement to his champion, came the thought that here perhaps Abe had met his match. A sudden lightning-like shift of the hunter's grip and a sharp heave of his shoulders brought the tall youngster to earth yet again, and the watchers could see that this time Abe was hard put to it to defend himself. He was on his right side, with the powerful Crockett partly on top of him, struggling to turn him with a half nelson—a hold in which the hunter's left arm was used as a lever under Abe's left arm and around the back of his neck.

The Hoosier's long legs were spread in a wide V to brace him, and he seemed to be making a last desperate resistance against a defeat he could not avoid.

"Gosh," groaned Tad, as he saw Abe's shoulders slowly giving.

"Hol' on!" Allen breathed. "He ain't done yet."

And almost before the words had left his mouth, the whole complexion of the bout had changed. With a sudden tremendous twist, Abe rolled over to his right side, breaking the hold, and as he turned, his long, strong legs wound themselves swiftly about the hunter's middle.

"Hooray!" yelled Allen. "I was waitin' fer that. Watch, now, when he puts the clamps on!"

The Tennesseean strove fiercely to break loose, but those fence-rail legs of Abe's were as tough as hickory. He locked them at the ankles, and as his knees straightened, the hunter's breath came in short, hard gasps. And slowly Abe began to turn him over.

As the minutes passed, Crockett's endurance ebbed. He made one final try, fighting with the fury of a wildcat to escape from the vise in which he was gripped. Then as his muscles relaxed, his young antagonist pressed him downward with his shoulders squarely on the ground.

"Say ''nough'?" panted Abe. But Crockett had no breath to speak. He moved his head in a weary gesture of assent.

The Indiana boy unwound his legs and got up, stiffly, reaching out a hand to the defeated bear-hunter. Crockett stumbled to his feet and stood feeling gingerly of his ribs.

"Yuh-yuh—you keep the b'ar!" he gasped when enough of his wind returned, and a sort of rueful grin wrinkled his leather-brown face.

The wrestlers were both in such perfect condition that they were soon feeling as fit as ever. Abe turned from his playful mauling of the bear cub to speak to his late opponent. "We didn't say, at the start-off, whether this yere match was one fall or best two out o' three," he said. "What say—want to try another?"

"No, sir," replied the hunter promptly. "That's mighty square of you, but I reckon I know when I'm beat. I've wrastled with plenty o' good ones an' never been thrown till now. But I never tackled a feller as strong as you, nor as long. All arms an' legs—iron legs, at that.

"Wal, boys," he cried, "what are ye—hungry? How 'bout some b'ar steak, cooked fresh, Injun fashion?"

The sun was getting low and all of the flatboat hands had good appetites. They went to work with a will, therefore, brought in dry wood by the armful, and soon were broiling the meat on green sticks over a hot fire.

It was Tad's first taste of bear, and he was not at all sure he liked it at the start. But soon he was eating it like the rest, with gusto. Allen brought a pan and some cups down from the boat, and they finished with a round of tea.

Crockett smacked his lips over the steaming

beverage. "Boy, howdy!" said he. "I ain't had a cup fer close to a month. This b'ar-huntin' is a good trade, but it makes ye give up a lot o' refinements.

"Ye know," he said, and hesitated, blushing a little, "I was up to Washington fer the last term o' Congress—sent up to represent the folks in this part o' Tennessee. But I never could git accustomed to city ways. I'd git to feelin' jest about starved fer a mess o' b'ar's meat every once in so often. An' it's the same way now I'm back home here, roamin' through the woods an' the cane-brake; I git a hankerin' sometimes fer jelly-cake an' tea.

"Ever thought about goin' in fer politics, Longshanks?"

It was Abe's turn to blush. "I've thought about a heap o' things," he answered gruffly. "Politics, fer one, because I like to make speeches an' get a crowd to listen to me. What I'd like to be most, though, is a good lawyer."

Allen haw-hawed loudly at this confession, but Davy Crockett listened with respect.

"I'll wager you'll git thar," he nodded. "Though I don't hold much with lawyers, myself. They're too slick—always up to some crooked business."

Abe warmed up at once. "That's exactly the reason," said he. "I want to be a good enough lawyer to beat some o' the smart ones at their own game. A good lawyer kin be a powerful lot o' help to folks that's in trouble."

He settled down again in his place before the fire, crossing his long legs and chuckling reminiscently as he looked at Allen. "Puts me in mind of old Jeff Slocum," said he. "A lot of us boys saw him lyin' side o' the road one blizzardy night. He'd been thrown out o' the tavern an hour before an' started fer home too drunk to stagger. We all thought 'twas jest a log o' wood or some brush that the snow was beginnin' to cover, but I wasn't dead sure an' went back. Thar he lay, half drifted over, an' right on the edge o' freezin'. So I threw him over my shoulder an' lugged him home to his cabin. I got a fire goin' an' rubbed him with snow an' finally thawed him out, an' thanks to all the red-eye he'd drunk, he was 'round in a week, right as ever.

"But come summer he got in trouble again, an' that time I couldn't help him a particle. Seems like some o' his shoats got into Newt Padgett's bean-patch an' dug things up pretty general. An' Newt, bein' the meanest man on the whole creek, hauled Jeff into court. He got a judgment fer more'n Jeff ever owned, spite o' the fact that the trouble all rose from Newt bein' too mean to keep his fences up.

"I sure wished right then that I was a lawyer," Abe finished. "I believe I could have saved Jeff's bacon."

"You've got the right idee," said the bear-hunter. "Whar the land is bein' settled up so fast, thar's bound to be more an' more law, and with it more lawyers. An' this country sure needs the kind o' lawyers that you aim to be, 'stid o' the other kind.

"Speakin' fer myself, I don't keer so much about law as I do about independence. When I've got the ol' rifle along I don't need laws to protect me. Here in Tennessee it's gittin' 'most too civilized now. I don't take no comfort when I shoot, fer fear I'll hit some one. I've been thinkin' some about goin' up the Missouri or down Mexico way. As long as thar's more b'ars than people, I kin stand 'most any sort o' country. But soon as the folks ketches up on the b'ars, I figger it's gittin' too crowded."

Crockett rose and stretched his powerful frame.

"Sun's a-settin' an' I've got 'most ten miles to travel back to my camp," he said. "Much obleeged fer your company an' fer the wrastlin' lesson. If you aim to push on tonight, you'll be out o' this cut within two mile, an' it's open river fer quite a ways below.''

They bade him farewell and saw him slip into the tangled cane silently as an Indian, the big dogs trotting at his heels. Then they boarded the flatboat once more, and pushed off.

Tad, searching among the gear in the *Katy Roby's* hold, found a light chain which he substituted for the rope about the cub's neck, and fastened him to a staple amidships, with a pile of dry grass for a bed.

The little black fellow pulled comically at the chain with his paws, tested its length by prowling back and forth a few times, and finally curled up in his nest for a nap. Tad left him snoring and tiptoed forward where Abe was pulling at the oars.

The tall Hoosier worked awhile in silence, his face somber in the gathering dusk. Then a grin twisted the corners of his big mouth. ''Lucky thing fer me this Crockett feller didn't take me up on another fall,'' said he. ''I was closer to gittin' my deserts that time than I ever remember. He'd have thrown me sure, I reckon. Golly, what a man!''

Tad stoutly pooh-poohed the idea that Davy

Crockett, or any other human, could take the measure of his hero. But Abe smiled and shook his head.

" 'Tain't jest that he was strong,'' he explained. "There's plenty o' big, powerful men. But I never hooked up with one that was faster on his feet or had more grit.''

Night had fallen when they reached the end of the cut, and they could see little of the river below except a wide, shadowy expanse of water with indistinct lines of shore receding on either hand.

"Sleepy, Tad?'' asked Abe. "If ye ain't, we'd better keep a double look-out fer snags an' sand-reefs. I'm a-goin' right on till Allen wakes up an' spells me.''

The boy took up his position squatting in the bow, his gaze straining into the dark ahead. There was no noise except the lap of the hurrying river around the flatboat's sides and the occasional soft creak of the tholepins. The deck heaved slightly, with a steady, breathing motion, as Abe's moccasins trod backward and forward, and the long sweeps pulled through the water.

Tad, his fancy thrilled at first by the vast loneliness around them and the sense of mystery and adventure in their silent downward voyage, began to feel sleepy after an hour or two. He shifted

his position again and again, to shake himself
awake, but his head would nod in spite of all his
efforts.

Suddenly there came sounds from the left bank,
half a mile away, that made him start bolt upright,
wide awake and listening.

A shout carried across the water, menacing and
sharp. There was an interval of a few seconds and
then an eager whimper reached them, followed by
a deep, bell-like tone—the baying of a hound.
Lights appeared, glimmering in jerky movements
along the shore. Another shout or two followed,
and then everything was quiet. The lights disappeared one by one, and the desolate, brooding
dark settled once more over the face of the river.

"What was it, Abe?" whispered the boy.

"Dunno," said Abe. "No way o' tellin'. But it
sure did give me the cold creeps; didn't it you?"

"Yes," shivered Tad. He was no longer sleepy.
With every sense on the alert, he watched the dim
banks and the dusky water ahead. Thoughts of the
terrible Murrell and other cold-blooded rogues of
the river crossed his mind. For nearly half an hour
he expected momentarily to see danger of some
kind develop. Then, just as he was lulling himself
into a sense of security, another startling thing
happened.

Directly in their path ahead, Tad thought he made out a dark object drifting with the current. He scrambled to his knees, peering fixedly at the spot, and Abe stopped rowing. ''What d'ye see?'' asked the big oarsman in a low voice.

''Just a floating log, I think,'' Tad whispered, ''only I thought I saw it move.''

The dark object was only a dozen yards away now, and they could distinguish the outline of an uprooted tree trunk. Abe was just changing the flatboat's course with a vigorous pull on the starboard oar when Tad gave a sudden exclamation. A part of the log had seemed to separate from the main trunk and had slid off with a considerable splash into the river.

''Look!'' cried Tad, pointing to the other side of the floating snag. A dark, round object which had been drawing rapidly away to the right disappeared under water at the boy's exclamation. And though they watched intently while they passed the log, and for many minutes after, they had no further glimpse of it.

''That must have been a man, swimmin','' said Abe at length. ''Too big fer a muskrat or a turtle. Didn't look like a panther nor a b'ar. Runaway slave, I reckon. Wal, the pore devil needn't have been so scairt of us.''

Allen came forward, wakened by the talk, and heard their story. ''That's probably what the commotion on shore was about,'' he said. ''You fellers is both tired, so I'll take her down awhile, jest driftin'. Won't need a look-out that way.''

And Abe and Tad, going aft to their blankets, were soundly sleeping within ten minutes.

CHAPTER IX

THE LITTLE BEAR took very kindly to his new home. He slept well and rose to stretch himself hungrily when the first beam of sunlight came over the brown water. Softly he padded about the half circle of which his chain was the radius, but there seemed to be nothing to eat within reach. Rolled up in a blanket near by, however, he found one of the queer-smelling two-legged creatures that had been kind to him the day before, and being of an inquisitive turn of mind he immediately thrust a moist little black snout between the blanket and the sleeper's neck.

Tad, awakened by the touch of the cub's cold nose, let out a squeal and rolled violently over on to Abe, who woke in his turn, and scrambled up, reaching for an ax.

"Haw!" roared Allen. "Haw, haw, haw! Might think the ol' Scratch himself was arter ye! Wal, he got ye up anyhow."

Abe and Tad rubbed their eyes and joined sheepishly in the laughter. And the cub, after looking at them all solemnly, returned to his investigation of Tad's blanket.

"This little feller's got to have a name," chuckled Abe. "He acts like he's adopted us fer keeps, an' if he's goin' to be a full-fledged hand we'll have to call him somethin'."

"Let's christen him Poke," said Tad. "He's always into everything." And Poke was his name from that moment on.

Allen had tied up to the shore after midnight and risen to start again at dawn. Now they were drifting steadily down the middle of a reach where there was no immediate occasion for steering, and Allen sat down with the others amidships at breakfast. He was weary and cross from his vigil at the sweep.

"See here," he demanded as Poke looked up hopefully after his third helping of johnny-cake, "how in Tarnation are we ever a-goin' to feed this brute? We ain't provisioned fer but two hands, an' this b'ar eats more'n a grown man."

Abe went on calmly with his breakfast. "I didn't save him an' wrastle fer him jest to throw him back in the river," he said. "Here, he kin have mine." And placing his own piece of corn-bread in front of the greedy little bear, he rose, whistling, to take up his morning's labor at the bow oars.

"Tad," he called, from the foredeck, "you're

the rightful owner of this b'ar. S'pose you git out that hand-line an' bait it an' see if ye can't save the rations by puttin' us on a fish diet fer a day or two.''

The boy was only too glad to try. He had done some fishing farther up the river, but without any notable results.

"Ought to bite good, today," said Allen, sniffing the breeze with a knowing air. "Feels like it's comin' on to rain, soon—tonight, mebbe. That'll bring 'em up."

Tad dropped his baited hook over the side and sat down comfortably, prepared for a tedious wait. But scarcely had the length of the line run out, when he felt such a tug on the other end that it nearly pulled him overboard. He held fast, bracing his feet, and shouted excitedly for aid. Allen took hold with him.

"Huh," he grunted. "Must be snagged, I reckon. Wal, we can't afford to lose the hook. Nothin' for it but pull her in."

Together they hauled the line aboard hand over hand. There seemed to be a heavy, inert weight attached to it.

"Golly," growled Allen, "all this work jest to turn loose a durned ol' water-logged root or somethin'!"

But Tad was still pulling manfully. "Look!" he

cried. "It's no snag—it's a fish—a catfish—great jumping catamounts, what a fish! How're we going to land him?"

Allen gave one astounded glance over the side and dashed for the bucket-hook, a stout sapling with an upward-forking branch at the lower end. While Tad held the nose of the big fish at the surface, Allen thrust down the wooden hook and brought it up under one of the gills. "Now," he cried, "both together, heave!"

And out of the water came a great, grizzled mud cat, so heavy that it took all their strength to haul him over the gunwale. The big fish thrashed ponderously about for a moment and then lay quiet.

"He's more'n four foot long," estimated Allen, "an' he'll tip seventy-five pound if he will an ounce. By gum, that's the biggest ol' catfish I ever caught."

"*You* caught!" snorted Abe, ambling aft to view the prize. "All the claim you've got on this fish is that you're goin' to cook him. This is Tad's fish."

He looked the catch over with an appraising eye. "Pretty fair-sized catfish fer such a young one," he remarked. "He's only about forty year old. You kin tell by the whiskers. His ain't even turned gray yet."

"Humph!" grunted Allen suspiciously.

"'Course," Abe went on, "you ain't had the opportunities for observin' catfish that I've been favored with. When I was workin' on the Anderson Creek ferry, up on the Ohio, there was an old fisherman that used to set thar in his boat day after day. He had two half-inch hemp ropes over the side. One was his anchor rope an' the other was his line. He never caught any small fish because on the end o' this line he used the hook off an ox-chain, baited with a half a ham.

"One day he let out a holler we could hear clear across the Ohio, an' we saw him wavin' his arms an' workin' like all git out. Then by 'n' by he come a-rowin' over our way. It was slow pullin', an' the stern o' the skiff was 'way down in the water, with the bow half out. When he got alongside we saw a real fish. The ol' feller had hauled him in till his nose was up against the stern, an' then lashed the rope to a thwart, an' hit him in the head with an ax. We helped him reach the landin' an' rigged a tackle an' fall, an' with two teams o' horses we managed to git the critter on shore.

"Eh? What did he weigh? Wal, now I don't jest quite recollect, but it was either four hundred and eighty-five pound or five hundred and eighty-four —my memory don't run to figgers. The real in-

terestin' part was his age. Riveted into his tail
was a brass plate, marked with a man's name an'
the year 1705. Seems like this ol' fisherman's
grandfather had caught the fish 'way back more'n
a hundred years ago an' marked him an' turned
him loose.

"Talk about whiskers—why, this one had a full
beard, jest as white as snow, an' I reckon his eyes
had gone back on him in his old age, fer he wore
a pair o' heavy-bowed spectacles."

"The fish?" asked Tad, gaping with astonishment.

"No," chuckled Abe, "the grandfather." And
he returned to his oars.

"Humph!" said Allen again, this time with a
real snort. "Whar you ever got the name of 'Honest Abe' is more'n I know. Honest! Why, thar
ain't a bigger liar from the Falls o' the Ohio to the
Gulf o' Mexico!"

They skinned the huge mud cat and cut it in two,
putting the larger part in a cool place, wrapped
in wet weeds. Tad was just building the fire pre-
paratory to cooking the rest of the fish, when Abe
spoke suddenly from the forward deck.

"Look astern, thar, boys," he said. They stood
up, their eyes sweeping the river to the north.
There were the usual two or three flatboats in the

distance and the smoke of a steamer above the last bend. But less than a quarter of a mile behind them, and drawing rapidly nearer, they saw a big rowboat with oars flashing in quick rhythm along its sides.

As the craft approached, it swung out a little to one side, and they saw that it was a good-sized barge, rowed by six powerful negroes. Four white men sat in the stern sheets, cradling shot-guns in the crook of their arms. They drew up alongside the *Katy Roby,* perhaps twenty yards distant, and at a word of command the blacks rested on their oars. For a moment the occupants of the two boats studied each other in silence. The white men aboard the barge were dressed in the elegant, careless fashion of southern planters. Their faces were unsmiling, very polite, very hard-eyed.

One of them nodded. ''We're out after a runaway nigger,'' he said, in an even tone. ''Maybe you can tell us where he is, suh.''

Abe straightened up, towering from the fore deck like a young Goliath. His voice had the ring of steel in it, and his speech, as always at tense moments, was singularly free from the slipshod backwoods dialect.

''He's not aboard here,'' he answered, ''and as far as we know we haven't seen him.''

There were whispers among the men in the barge. Then the spokesman, with another look at Abe, made an impatient gesture to the rowers, and the craft was speedily under way once more.

"What did I tell ye last night?" said Allen, when they were out of earshot. "That's what all the noise was about on shore. They must ha' tracked him to the river with bloodhounds. Gosh all fishhooks, Abe! I figgered they was goin' to search us, sure. Did ye see them guns!"

"Yep," said Abe. "They could ha' done it fast 'nough if they'd wanted to."

The *Katy Roby* held her course all day, proceeding at the leisurely gait that seemed so well suited to her buxom lines. The sky grew more and more overcast, and by afternoon a steady drizzle of rain began to fall. There was little to do but stay under cover as much as possible, swap yarns, and play with Poke, now apparently quite at home in his new surroundings.

It was during Allen's trick at the oars, when Tad and Abe were lying under the shelter of a tarpaulin, that the younger boy brought up a subject always close to the surface of his mind.

"Abe," he said, "how long ought it to take that letter of mine to reach New Orleans?"

Abe put down the tattered copy of Shake-

speare's tragedies he was reading. "Let's see,"
he pondered. "That was a week ago yesterday we
went ashore, up thar. S'pose the steamboat happened along right off the next day, like the store
feller said. That would give a week—sartin sure—
that's time enough fer 'em to git to New Orleans,
easy. I'll jest wager your Paw is a-readin' that
letter an' congratulatin' hisself right this minute."

"Gee," sighed the boy, "I'll feel better when I
know for sure that he's got it and isn't worrying
any longer!"

It was well on in the afternoon and the dismal
sky was bringing an early dusk when they sighted
the barge once more, returning upstream. It
passed fairly close, the oars still beating in brisk
time against the current. But this time there was a
fifth figure among the armed white men in the
stern. A big negro, his naked back and shoulders
gleaming darkly in the rain, crouched in the middle of the group. They could not see his face, but
there were terror and despair in every line of his
cowering body.

As they watched the boat they saw it veer over
in the direction of a small island they had passed
in midstream a mile or so above.

''That's whar they'll fix him,'' said Allen grimly.

''What do you mean—kill him?'' asked Tad.

''Not a mite of it,'' the other replied. ''Ye don't ketch them fellers throwin' away a thousand dollars. They'll make him wish he hadn't, though. The way I've heard tell about it, they'll likely start a bonfire, thar on the island, an' take a gunbar'l, or mebbe a reg'lar iron made fer the job, an' burn a big mark on to his chest an' arms. Arter he gits well that brand'll allers be on him, so the overseers kin watch him extra keerful an' give him a double dose o' the whip if he looks sideways.''

''Yes,'' said Abe, sober-faced, ''as fur as he's concerned, he'd be a heap better off dead.''

They tied up to a big cottonwood on the Arkansas side, that night, and Tad lay a long time awake, listening to the ceaseless thud of the rain on wet planking and dripping canvas. The thought of the runaway negro, captured after his break for freedom and dragged back to the torture, seemed to haunt him. At last the monotone of the rain was broken by a shivery squall—the cry of a wildcat, somewhere back in the brush. Poke roused himself with an uneasy grunt, and Tad rolled over, pulling the blanket tighter about him.

"That you, Tad?" came Abe's low voice. "I can't git comfortable, neither. That poor devil gittin' caught that way 'pears to have upsot me. Well, thar ain't much we kin do about it. Let's go to sleep."

And whether Abe was successful himself or not, his suggestion seemed to be all that Tad needed, for he dropped off at once into deep slumber.

The rain continued falling steadily for the next two days, and with it the water began to rise. They watched it climb inch by inch as they drifted south, till the yellow tide was swirling half-way up the tree trunks and broadening into vast lakes in the lower lands.

It was difficult, often, to pick out the course of the main river, for except where lines of cottonwoods fringed the banks, it was all one dreary expanse under the sullen beat of the rain.

Everything was wet—clothes, blankets, food. Even Allen's banjo was temporarily out of commission. The boys' spirits flagged, and if it had not been for the antics of the little bear and an occasional story from Abe, their party would have been glum indeed.

At last, in the late afternoon of the second day, there was a shift in the wind and the clouds began to break, with hazy shafts of pink and gold streaming through. In the midst of their jubilation, Allen, who had the steering-oar, pointed a finger toward the Tennessee shore.

"Look," he cried, "a steamboat landin' an' houses! That's Memphis, boys, sure as you're born!" And leaning heavily against the sweep, he swung the flatboat's bow over toward the town.

CHAPTER X

Memphis, in 1828, was little more than a raw hamlet straggling along the river. It had a big landing-stage for steamers and a series of smaller wharves where the arks and keel boats from upstream could tie up. There were half a hundred craft of all sorts and sizes hitched to the mooring-posts when the *Katy Roby* drew alongside, for nearly every flatboat crew made a stop of a day or a night at Memphis. It was the largest town between St. Louis and New Orleans and handled a considerable commerce with the back country.

The boys worked the boat's nose in between other broadhorns until they could get a rope fast, and Allen retired to the shelter amidships to shave and spruce himself up.

"Reckon I'll step ashore an' see what prices they're offerin' fer corn an' pork," he remarked, endeavoring to part his hair with the aid of a piece of broken mirror.

"Yes," said Abe, "an' don't fergit to take note o' the number o' purty gals an' the color o' their dresses. Tad an' me, we'll stick along here an' teach this no-'count Poke some new tricks."

They cooked supper, and as Allen did not return at dusk, they ate it, sitting together on the edge of the fore deck. There were numerous boatmen joking, swearing, and passing the time of day in the craft about them. Several of the crews were familiar to them from earlier meetings along the river, and there was much cheerful banter about Abe's towering frame. He took it all with his customary grin and gave them as good as they sent.

"Say, Hoosier," yelled one jolly-looking, red-bearded keel-boat man, "how long are them shanks o' yourn, anyhow?"

"Jest the proper length," Abe returned. "They're jest exactly long enough to reach the ground."

Gradually the talk and laughter quieted down as darkness fell. By nine o'clock the river front was quiet except for the gurgle of the high water sweeping past and an occasional burst of song from roisterers in the town.

Abe waited patiently until some time close to midnight. Then he nudged the drowsy Tad awake and told him to mind the boat while he went ashore after Allen.

Tad succeeded in propping his eyes open for half an hour, and at the end of that time he saw a huge, dim shape lurching along the dock. As it reached the bow of the *Katy Roby* it became recognizable as Abe, carrying a limp body over his shoulder.

Tad leaped up, startled.

"What is it—is Allen hurt?" he whispered.

"No," Abe replied, quietly. "He's drunk."

They took off some of his clothes and wrapped him in his blanket. Then Abe stretched his big arms and spat over the gunwale disgustedly.

"There's no law to stop a feller from makin' a fool of himself," he remarked. "Only ye'd think plain common sense ought to tell him." And with that they went to bed.

Allen made a very unheroic figure next morning. His complexion was a sort of greenish yellow, and he refused all food with groans.

"What about prices on the cargo?" Abe asked him. "Want to stay an' unload some?"

Allen shook his head. "Too cheap," said he. "Let's hold the stuff fer New Orleans an' git thar as soon as we kin." Whereupon he rolled over once more and lay in a miserable heap while Abe and Tad made preparations for departure.

They needed sugar and white flour, and before casting off, Abe made a hurried trip up into the town to get them.

When he came back his face was grave.

"They say there's a heap o' damage from the high water all along below here," he told Tad. "We'll have to watch sharp and help folks out whar we kin. An' then I heard another piece o' news. They say this outlaw John Murrell is back from up river, an' him an' his gang are startin' to make life miserable fer the planters betwixt here an' Natchez. The storekeeper wanted to skeer me, I reckon. He claimed Murrell would sink a flatboat an' drown the crew fer a ten-dollar note. But I don't pay much heed to that sort o' talk.

"An' anyhow, if he wants our ten dollars, let him try it. I'd sort o' like to see Mr. Murrell fer myself an' find out if he's such a terrible feller."

Tad was not quite so sure he wanted to test the notorious outlaw's mettle, but he agreed that it might be thrilling to get a glimpse of him.

They got off before the morning was far advanced, and soon overtook some of the other flatboats which had started before them. Abe took a keen delight in overhauling them, one after another, and tossing back a gibe or two at each vessel they passed.

At length there was only one craft left in sight ahead of them—a long, trimly-built keel-boat, with lines that were almost graceful compared to those of the *Katy Roby*. She was making good headway, due to the efforts of a husky bow-oarsman, but Abe's extra-long sweeps and the tremendous power he put into his stroke were rapidly eating up the distance between the two boats.

Just as the bow of the broadhorn drew even with her rival's steering-oar, another figure sprang to the fore deck of the keel-boat. It was the big red-bearded river-man who had asked Abe about the length of his legs. He swung an arm in vigorous gesture, and his voice roared out across the water.

"Git down from thar, ye lousy swab," he cried to the oarsman. "Let somebody pull that knows a sweep from a shovel."

The rower hastened to surrender the great, clumsy oars and scramble down, out of the way. And then indeed began a race! The slenderer lines of the keel-boat gave her a slight advantage, which Abe had to overcome by the sheer force of his strokes. During that moment while the oars were changing hands, the tall Indiana boy quickened the beat of his swing and succeeded in pulling up till he was a shade ahead of the other craft. From this point he could watch his rival without turning his head, while the redbeard was forced to crane his neck in order to see what Abe was doing.

So they went, side by side, for the best part of a mile, the muddy water churning in yellow foam behind them. The other four men in the keel-boat's crew bellowed constant encouragement to their mate, and one of them seized the steering-sweep, sculling from side to side to help them along. Tad saw this maneuver and promptly matched it by doing the same thing with the *Katy Roby's* stern oar.

At the end of ten minutes the furious pace began to tell on the red-whiskered rower. He was wilting visibly, while Abe, who had been at it for more than an hour, was still pulling as strongly as ever.

One of the keel-boat men climbed to the fore deck and held a whisky jug to the lips of his champion. This measure seemed to put new vigor into him for about ten strokes. Then he stumbled and caught a crab, and the race was over.

Abe pulled far enough ahead so that there should be no doubt about it, then waited, resting on his oars.

He was panting hard, but his grin made him look anything but exhausted. As Tad came forward, he mopped his forehead with his sleeve.

"Son," said he, between breaths, "don't ever

let the other feller know you're as tired as he is. If he thinks you're still fresh he'll quit.''

After that they drifted for a while, and toward noon the big keel-boat dropped down abreast of them again. The ruddy-bearded captain steered close enough for conversation and grinned sociably as he spoke.

''Whar you from?'' he asked.

Abe told him and came back with a similar question.

''We're bringin' a load o' furs down from St. Louis,'' answered the keel-boat skipper. ''Ol' Man Carillon, he's scairt to ship by steamboat—'fraid they'll blow up. So he still sends his furs this way. More'n a thousand prime beaver skins we've got, an' plenty of other kinds besides. That'd be a haul worth even John Murrell's time, eh? I've got two extra men in the crew jest 'count o' him an' his gang.''

''They tell me he's back,'' said Abe.

''Sure thing,'' replied the other. ''He was layin' low fer a couple o' months, up river, but this last week he's been seen ridin' the roads on that three-stockin' hoss o' his—him an' Bull Whaley an' Sam Jukes. That means thar's some sort o' devilment a-bilin'.''

''Well,'' Abe answered, ''jes' so he stays on horseback an' don't come meddlin' with river folks, he'll mebbe keep a whole skin.''

The keel-boat left them some distance astern while Abe was getting dinner, but later in the day they sighted it again, and for the next forty-eight hours the two craft were rarely more than a few miles apart.

Allen did not wake up until nearly dark, and even then he had little stomach for the sizzling hog-meat that Abe was frying. Next morning, however, he was feeling like himself once more, and was even ready to brag about his experiences ashore in Memphis, if Abe's cutting sarcasm had not quieted him.

They went down swiftly on the flood-water, twisting and turning through new channels, and dashing through chutes where the river had straightened its course and ran like a mill race. Occasionally they saw the roofs of submerged cabins, and once or twice, when there seemed a chance that people might be left in them, they stopped to see if they could be of any help. In one house, floating with a gable end thrust up at a crazy angle, they saw the body of a drowned woman caught by the clothing to a window frame and trailing pitifully in the water. But aside from that they found no human trace in all the desolate welter of the river.

On the third day after leaving Memphis they passed the mouth of a great river—the Arkansas —a raging tide that bore witness to heavy floods in the back country.

For miles below, the surface of the Mississippi was littered with gruesome débris. There were limbs of trees, parts of houses, bloated bodies of farm animals. A huge flock of buzzards circled and settled, on tilting black wings, and a stench of death filled the air.

Once, when Tad was perched high astern, swinging the steering-oar, he caught sight of the carcass of a pig a little distance off. And even as he watched, it was suddenly yanked under, leaving only a gurgling eddy in the stream.

The St. Louis keel-boat was not far away, and her red-bearded captain called across to Tad.

"Did ye see that?" he cried. "Big alligator done it. We'll find lots of 'em below here."

Sure enough, as they cast off next morning from the high bank topped with cottonwoods where they had spent the night, a row of gnarled gray logs below them came alive, turned with a swish of tails, and went lumbering into the water.

''Don't reckon we'll be so keen to go swimmin', from here down,'' Abe chuckled.

There were other signs that told them they had come into the real South. Cotton plantations replaced the woods and squatters' farms on the higher ground. Broad, stout levees held the river in check for miles along the steaming bottom lands. The weather was uncomfortably hot, even in the scanty costumes which the boys wore. They kept out of the sun as much as possible during the heat of the day, but their faces, arms, and ankles were burned the color of an Indian's. Abe, who had been reading *Othello*, told Allen solemnly that he looked like the Moor of Venice.

Three days after they passed the Arkansas mouth, they sighted Vicksburg, a white town nestled in the crook of a bend, with water above the top of the landings and washing over the lowest street.

Allen was ready for another adventure ashore, but Abe prevailed on him to wait.

''Ye don't figger the price o' pork has gone up much since we left Memphis, do ye?'' said the lanky bow oarsman scornfully. ''After the spectacle ye made o' yerself up thar, I should think ye'd want to look the other way if a town so much as came in sight.''

"That whisky must ha' had pizen in it," Allen muttered. But he had very little more to say until they had left the landing astern.

"Oh, well," he remarked at length, "we'll be down to Natchez in another day or two, an' I reckon we'll need some more provisions by then. Natchez-under-the-Hill!" He pronounced the name of the town with a certain relish. "The toughest landin' on the whole river. I sure aim to see the sights of that place."

"The toughest sight you'll see," said Abe firmly, "will be the flat o' my hand, unless you behave yourself mighty well from here down."

The crest of the high water had passed, and the river was gradually receding as they drifted southward. Along the bluffs on the Mississippi side they watched a panorama of cotton plantations, half screened by glossy-leaved magnolias in the gardens of the big white houses.

This was a rich country—a land of fabulous ease and prosperity, it seemed to the two Hoosiers. Even Tad, who had seen plenty of wealth in the Eastern cities, was amazed by the glimpses they got of the luxurious planters' life.

Once they passed a barge trimly painted in green and white, with cushions and trailing silks over the stern. It was rowed by four negroes, and its passengers were a lovely lady in a flowered bonnet, a big, jolly, fair-haired man, and a little girl with golden curls.

The barge stopped at a private landing where a shining barouche with two high-headed bay horses was waiting. Other horses, saddled and held by negro grooms, stood near, and an elegantly dressed gentleman and lady strolled down to the landing to greet the visitors. The crew of the flatboat, drifting out of sight, caught a chime of fairy-like laughter that followed them around the bend.

"Jiminy!" sighed Allen. "This is the section to live in, all right. Niggers to wait on ye, an' fine hosses, an' summer all the year 'round!"

"I dunno," said Abe, thoughtfully. "It's grand fer the folks that owns the niggers, but how about these poor whites, along the bottoms an' back in the brush? They ain't as well off as you an' your Paw, by a long shot. The South is fine, but it's no country fer folks that ain't born rich."

There were two more drowsy, uneventful days of drifting, and then at dusk they came in sight of Natchez. It was the beginning of an experience that Tad was never to forget as long as he lived.

There was a terrifying beauty over the river that night. A strange green light had overspread the sky after sunset, and in it every detail of the bank and the bluff stood out with unearthly clearness. The air was sultry, with no hint of the breeze that usually ruffled the water at evening. From a reedy place, shadowed by moss-draped live oaks, a pair of great white egrets rose and winged silently away to the northward.

They saw a church spire above the trees at the top of the bluff, and then, low in the shadow along the waterside, the outlines of shacks and houses, with a swarm of flatboats moored to the levee. A thin tinkle of music reached their ears, and as they drew closer it resolved itself into the squeak of fiddles and the throb of banjos.

They found a place to tie their craft, down at the lower end of the line, near the steamboat landing, and hardly had they made the ropes fast when a growl of thunder drowned out the music. A wind sprang up, blowing from the south, and the sky grew dark with scudding clouds.

A sudden foreboding filled Tad. From that instant he had a dread of Natchez-under-the-Hill.

CHAPTER XI

THE STORM struck hard, lashing the muddy water high along the levee and tossing the broadhorns at their moorings. After the furious wind came rain in a deluge that drenched the boys under their hastily erected tarpaulins. And after the rain a pitch-black, sodden night.

A few lights glowed feebly in the town, and the music struck up again after a while, but even Allen was too damp and dispirited to feel like going ashore. They got a fire started on the wet hearth, and huddling around it, finally went to sleep.

The sun was shining in the morning and all along the waterfront a bustle of activity began. Boatmen clambered across the decks of neighboring craft to buy or sell goods or visit acquaintances. There was a constant noise of laughing, shouting, swearing, and fighting.

The fiddles began their monotonous squeaking once more in the levee saloons, and Allen began to cast a restless eye shoreward, but Abe found plenty for them all to do aboard the *Katy Roby.* They cooked and ate breakfast, swabbed the decks, and spread out their bedding to dry in the sun. They watched a big, new steamboat, the *Tecumseh,* swing in to the landing, her bow a bare thirty feet from them when she made her mooring.

"That's the fastest boat on the river," they heard a near-by ark-captain say. "She's got new-fangled boilers with more steam pressure on 'em than the *Amazon,* even. An' they say her cap'n is out to break all records to Louisville this trip."

From the speed with which her darky deck hands rolled molasses hogsheads aboard, it could be seen that some of the excitement of her race up-river had got into their blood.

A group of fastidiously dressed passengers, thronging her upper decks, looked down with laughing interest at the scene on the landing. The men were holding watches and laying wagers on the time of the steamer's departure. In less than half an hour the last huge barrel was in place on the forward cargo deck and the mate cried his "All aboard," as the negroes ran the gangplank in. With a clang of bells the big boat's paddles churned the water and she backed out, wheeling into the current.

Tad, looking up a little wistfully at her gleaming brass and freshly painted upper works, watched her whole magnificent length sweep by. And then suddenly he gripped the gunwale of the flatboat and stared open-mouthed. For high up on the hurricane deck, astern, he had seen a solitary figure—a big middle-aged man with a beaver hat and a familiar set to the shoulders. The man was just turning to leave the rail and he was unable to get a good view of his face, but he was almost sure . . . "Dad!" he screamed, with all the voice he could muster, "Dad!"

There had been a feather of white steam up aloft on the *Tecumseh's* funnel when he started to shout, and as he launched his cry a deafening blast of the whistle came, drowning him out.

Another long-drawn hoot and two short ones followed. Before they were finished, the steamboat was a hundred yards away, and the man who looked like Tad's father had vanished down the companionway. The boy had a great lump in his throat as he turned away. He stumbled aft and sat down beside Poke, blinking his eyes fast to keep back the unmanly tears.

Abe had heard him shout and now came over to stand behind him, dropping a big hand casually on his shoulder.

"Reckon that was your father?" he asked.

Tad nodded. "I couldn't be sure," he answered, "but it looked a lot like him."

"Wal," said Abe, "I know how ye feel, right enough, but don't take it too hard. He'll be back in New Orleans to meet ye. Didn't ye tell him in yer letter that we'd be thar next week?"

"Sure," Tad replied. "Only he must be pretty worried, or he wouldn't be on his way up to try to find me, now."

Allen had been up on the levee, watching the *Tecumseh's* departure and chatting with a crowd of flatboat men. Now he returned with the look of one bearing news.

"Hey, Tad," he called as he jumped aboard, "what was the name o' that boat that was expected in Shawneetown—the one the postmaster said he'd mail yer letter by?"

"The *Nancy Jones*," said Tad.

"That's what I thought," Allen nodded. "Wal, they tol' me up on the bank jest now that the *Nancy Jones* was blowed up two weeks ago in Vicksburg bend, an' lost with more'n half her passengers an' crew."

Tad's jaw dropped. "Then—then Dad doesn't even know I'm alive," he stammered. "No wonder he's on his way up the river."

In a few words Abe told Allen of Tad's momentary glimpse of the man on the steamer. ''Now the thing fer you to do,'' said he, turning to the boy, ''is to send another letter post-haste to New Orleans, so the folks thar kin reach him whar he's gone.''

''I'm goin' ashore,'' Allen volunteered. ''He kin come along an' fix up to send his letter whiles I transact some business.''

Abe looked doubtful. ''All right,'' he agreed finally. But to Tad, as they prepared to leave the boat, he whispered, ''Keep an eye on him now, an' don't let him go in any places he shouldn't.''

They clambered to the levee top and walked through the thick black mud up the main street of the lower town. It was nearly noon, and Natchez was waking up for the day's work. Patrons by ones and twos were entering the various barrooms they passed. Gambling joints were rolling up shutters and dusting off tables. A few women, hard-faced and heavily painted, leered at them from doorways, and the dance-hall music droned on unceasingly.

A negro teamster directed them to the post office on a side street a few blocks from the river.

''Here you are,'' said Allen as they reached the entrance, and Tad would have gone in at once if his eye had not been caught by a notice posted in the dusty window. With growing excitement he stood before it, staring at the boldly-printed words. What he read was this:

To Whom It May Concern

A

REWARD OF $5,000

(Five thousand Dollars)
will be paid for
Information

leading to the recovery of my son, Thaddeus Hopkins, if alive, or of his body if dead.

This boy is 15 years old, of medium height and weight for his age, with light brown hair, blue eyes, and a ruddy complexion.

DISAPPEARED

from his cabin on the Steamboat *Ohio Belle,* somewhere between Owensboro, Kentucky, and the mouth of the Wabash River, on the night of April 8th, 1828.

Any one having news of his whereabouts should communicate immediately with

JEREMIAH HOPKINS,
26 St. Louis Street,
New Orleans, Louisiana.

"Allen!" Tad gasped. "Look at this!"

There was no answer. Swinging about in surprise, he found the street behind him empty. Only a lean yellow dog scratched for fleas in the middle of the dusty road.

Tad stared up and down the straggling rows of houses, bewildered at his companion's disappearance. Then his eye lit on two saloons across the way, and he knew at once where Allen had gone.

With Abe's parting injunction still fresh in his mind, he darted to the other side of the street and stood a moment in hesitation before the two doors. There was no way to tell which place Allen had entered except to go in himself and find out. He decided to try the right-hand building first.

The swinging half-door gave easily under his hand, and he stepped into a square, half-darkened room, with stained wooden tables and a long mahogany bar. There was no one in sight, and Tad hesitated a moment in the middle of the sanded floor, looking about him, disappointed. Then he caught the sound of voices and low laughter and saw that the door leading into the rear room stood slightly ajar. He fancied that it was Allen he heard, laughing over having given him the slip. Quickly he crossed the floor, pushed open the door, and walked through.

A glance showed him that there were only three men in the room, and that Allen was not one of them. At the right of the table was a broad, thick-necked, powerfully-built man with a tight stock and a red, angry-looking face. Next him sat a thin, sallow, rat-eyed fellow with a nervous affection that twitched one corner of his mouth downward into a sneer every second or two. The third member of the party slouched in his chair, a long, slim figure with a dark mustache, the upper part of his face shaded by the broad brim of his hat.

Each of the three had started slightly at the lad's abrupt entrance, and they now sat watching him with hostile eyes.

"I—I beg your pardon," said Tad. "I thought a friend of mine came in here." And he started to back out.

Suddenly the tall man with the black mustache was on his feet.

"Wait!" he ordered in a husky voice that struck terror to Tad's heart. "Stay where yo' are, suh."

But waiting was the last thing in the boy's mind. He had caught a glimpse of the man's face and his long, slim hands. It was the Wheeling gambler who had thrown him overboard from the *Ohio Belle*. With a sense of panic he turned and darted for the door, but he never reached it. A stool came whirling through the air and struck him in the back of the head, and down he went, his mind blanked out in a roaring gulf of darkness.

CHAPTER XII

The next thing Tad knew was a sensation of intense physical discomfort. His head throbbed fiercely, his wrists were chafed, and he lay, in a very painful position, face down, across the saddle-bow of a galloping horse. When his senses had cleared enough for him to remember what had happened, he tried to figure out where these desperadoes were taking him. But all that he could see, facing the ground, was the packed brown earth of the roadside and the flashing green of undergrowth beyond. He had a vague recollection of having been carried up a long, steep hill; so he supposed they must have climbed one of the roads that ran up along the bluff.

One other thing he noticed, and that seemed to increase the hazards of a situation which surely was already serious enough. As he swung, head down, he could watch the rhythmic movement of the horse's legs. Both forelegs white up to the knee—one hind leg white above the hock; three white "stockings." Where had he heard, in the last few days, of a "three-stocking" horse?

Then he remembered, and it came over him with

a sickening feeling that his life was worth very little, indeed. For the black-haired man who had once before tried to kill him and who now had him prisoner could be none other than the terrible John Murrell himself.

There were two other horses, one behind them and one ahead. Occasionally one of the riders would speak in a guarded voice, but for the most part they rode hard and in silence.

It might have been only half an hour that they traveled, after Tad regained consciousness. If so, it was the longest thirty minutes he had ever spent in his life.

At last, when it seemed as if he must cry out with pain if he were jolted any farther, his captor pulled the big horse, lathered and champing, to a stop.

Without ceremony he caught Tad by his shoulder and dropped him in a heap on the ground. The boy was helpless, his ankles and his wrists bound tightly. But his brain was still working, and after the first moment of relief he began looking around, to see, if possible, where he was.

Dense brush and tall trees flanked the narrow, grassy track on both sides, and there was no view that would show him how far they had come from the river.

The riders had stopped in front of a house that stood at the left of the road—a high, bleak frame building, with no trees in front to soften its harsh outline. The shutterless windows leered down like evil eyes on the unkempt, desolate dooryard. An unnatural silence hung about the premises. There was no singing of birds, and in the flat gray light of a cloudy noonday, the whole atmosphere of the place seemed lonely and sinister beyond compare.

The riders dismounted and talked together for a moment.

"Here," said the tall leader at length, "we can settle all that presently. You ride back down the road, Sam, and you, Bull, keep watch up the other way till I get him out of sight."

Tad heard the names with a shudder. He had guessed right, then. Bull Whaley and Sam Jukes were the chief lieutenants of the famous outlaw. He had heard of them and their cruelty from the keel-boat hands on the river.

Murrell stood looking down at him for a moment, an ironical smile twisting his pale face.

"I see you recall our havin' met before, suh," he said with his polite Southern drawl. "That's as it should be, fo' you are goin' to be my guest fo' a while. We'll see, now, if there are any quarters ready to receive you.''

He put two fingers between his lips and gave a singularly piercing whistle, so shrill that it hurt Tad's eardrums. In a few seconds the house door opened, and a gigantic negro, in the rough clothes of a field hand, ran down the steps.

Murrell looked from Tad to the huge negro and back at Tad again. He seemed to relish the situation. ''This,'' he explained to the boy, ''is Congo, my bodyguard. He was the son of a great African chief, and when they brought him off the slave ship he killed four men. They tortured him so that he will never hear or speak again. But I rode by at the right moment and saved him from death. At a sign from me he would pick you up now and tear you into forty pieces.''

The giant black seemed to sense what his master was saying, for he flexed his mighty fingers, and his sides shook with a great, silent laugh. Tad, looking into that cavernous mouth, saw that there was no tongue back of the gleaming white teeth, and the negro's ears had been cropped and mutilated in horrible fashion.

Murrell gestured toward the house and led the way to the steps, and Congo picked the boy up as easily as if he had been a baby. Through the doorway and along a narrow hall he carried him, and then at another signal from Murrell, he climbed with him up a flight of steep, rickety stairs. Opening a door at the top, he flung his burden down, and stood awaiting the further commands of his master.

Murrell nodded. When the negro had gone out, he stooped and dragged Tad a few feet into a shadowy corner. Here he picked up a heavy iron fetter attached to a three-foot chain, and clasped it around one of the boy's ankles. With a brass key taken from his pocket, he secured its ponderous lock.

"That and our hospitality," he chuckled, "ought to be plenty to keep you here. I'll let you have the use o' yo' hands to keep the fleas from bein' too familiar." So saying, he whipped out a clasp knife and cut the cords that had bound Tad's wrists and ankles. And with an exaggerated bow he went out, closing the door after him.

When the sound of his footsteps had died away at the bottom of the stairs, Tad raised himself to a sitting posture and looked about at his prison. In what he saw there was nothing to lighten the gloom of his desperate situation. The room was a long, narrow garret, lighted only by one window, at the farther end. Yellow, mildewed plaster was

dropping off the walls in flakes. The floor was a
mass of filth. Around him in the corner where he
sat were dirt and grease and foul-smelling rags,
and the whole place had a close, sickly odor that
nauseated him.

But Tad was not one to give up easily. He had
a stubborn sort of courage that rose to occasions
of this kind. And when he had conquered his first
feeling of illness, he set himself to test every
possible avenue of escape.

The chain attached to his ankle iron was heavy
and strong—a trace-chain from a wagon, he
judged. At the other end it was fastened to a huge
iron staple, driven solidly into one of the timbers
of the floor. A tug or two convinced him of the
utter futility of trying to pull it out. The fetter,
he was quite certain now, had been designed to
hold big, powerful men—the stolen slaves who
were said to be the special prey of Murrell and
his outlaw gang.

When he felt of the leg-iron itself, it seemed
large and loose about his ankle, though much too
small to allow his heel to pass through. His fingers
moved over the surface of the fetter and paused
suddenly in a deep, rough notch at the back, near
the hinge. With trembling hands he turned it as
far as he could and peered down at it through the

dim half-dusk. At some time or other the iron had been partly cut through by a file.

Tad's pulses leaped as he made this discovery. For a moment he thought he might finish what had been so well begun by some earlier prisoner. But as he searched about the floor in his corner he realized that there was nothing in sight that could possibly be used as an abrasive.

The afternoon dragged by with sickening slowness. The heat of the garret nearly suffocated him, and there was nothing to do but fight the flies and wait—for what, he did not know.

An intermittent drone of voices could be heard in the room downstairs. Gradually they grew louder—as the bottle was passed, Tad supposed—and he could even catch occasional words. Perhaps he would be able to overhear some of their plans. Crawling as far as the chain would permit, he stretched full length on his stomach, and laid an ear to the floor. As he did so, one of the boards moved a trifle under his hand. He touched it again and found it loose. By working his finger nails into the crack at one end he was able to lift it. The board was a short one that had been put in as a filler between two longer pieces. When Tad put his head down over the hole there were only thin lath and plaster between him and the room below.

Lying still and listening, he could now catch quite distinctly the louder parts of the conversation. There was a deep, angry voice which he recognized as that of Bull Whaley, and a thin whine that he thought must come from Sam Jukes. Murrell himself seemed to be saying very little.

"But five thousand dollars, man—why, that's the price of four or five good cotton niggers!" Whaley was roaring. "Don't the notice say 'dead or alive'? He's supposed to ha' been drowned, ain't he? Well," he finished triumphantly, "we kin fix that part of it easy enough."

"That's too risky," Jukes answered. "They'd be pretty sure to look into it if he was brought in dead. What I say is, let him be rescued by one of our New Orleans men. The boy won't ever suspect, an' his old man will be so thankful that he was delivered out o' the hands of the ruffians— meanin' you, Bull—that he'll pay the five thousand without a whimper. Let's see, now, LeGrand would be the chap to put it through. He's a good Creole an' stands well with the police."

"Huh!" Whaley grunted. "An' what'd Le-Grand want for the job? Half the reward, if I know him. No, sir, take him in dead, I says. There's more in it fer us that way."

Then Tad heard the husky drawl of the chief.

"Neither one of yo' ideas is wu'th the powder to blow it up, gentlemen," he said. "You're used to makin' small plans an' takin' small pickin's. Five thousand dollars is all either of you can see in this. I aim to get fifty thousand."

His words evidently left his hearers dumfounded. For a moment there was no sound. Then —"*Fifty* thousand!" both exclaimed together.

"That was what I said," Murrell returned. "This man Hopkins has offered a reward of five thousand. That means he is rich. He could scrape up, on his credit, all of fifty thousand dollars, and that is the sum I shall ask him to pay fo' the safe return of his son."

"Hold him fer ransom, eh?" said Whaley with a chuckle. "You win, Jack. I reckon if you sign the letter, they'll know they've got to pay or they'll never see him again."

"Yes, that's the plan, right enough," Jukes put in. "We'll have to fix up a good place for 'em to bring the money, though, so we can watch out for tricks."

"As to that," said Murrell, "I've worked out all the details. You know that island—" And here he dropped his voice too low for Tad's ears. The rest of the conversation was evidently held in an undertone, heads close together over the table, for try as he would, the boy could catch only a stray word now and then.

The sun had evidently broken through the clouds, for a slanting beam came through the cob-webs of the room's one window, which opened to-ward the west. And this feeble ray of light chanced to fall just inside the edge of the opening in the floor. It was a lucky chance for Tad. Glancing into the hole as he was about to crawl away, he saw something that made his heart jump into his throat. Quickly he reached down and brought it up into the light—a big, three-edged file.

The hole in the floor must have been the secret hiding-place used by that other prisoner, who had been taken away before his work on the fetter was finished.

Eagerly Tad felt the edges of the file. It was still sharp. He was just moving to a position where he could get at his ankle-iron when a step sounded on the stairs, and he had barely time to replace the tool in the aperture and cover it with the board. As he crawled back to his rags in the corner the door was opened and the giant slave, Congo, came in.

The negro set down a plate on which were some thick slices of buttered bread and a tin cup full of coffee. Tad waited for him to go, but he pointed down at the food and evidently expected to stay until it was finished. The boy had very little appetite, in spite of having tasted nothing since breakfast. He did manage, however, to eat two pieces of bread and gulp down the strong black coffee. Then an idea came to him. He had been wondering how he was to file his leg-iron without making too great a noise. If he could save the butter on the remaining piece of bread he might use it as a lubricant.

Picking up the slice he pretended to take a mouthful, meanwhile pushing the plate and cup toward Congo. The giant black stooped, picked them up, and stood for a moment grinning that terrible grin of his. Then he drew a forefinger slowly across his throat and rolled up his eyes till only the whites showed, in a ghastly pantomime of death. With this little token of farewell, he slipped through the door and bolted it on the outside.

Tad wasted no time in worrying over the meaning of the negro's signs. As soon as the footsteps had reached the bottom of the stairs he crept to his loose board and took the file from its hiding-place. In the fading twilight he could barely see the notch in the fetter, but it was easy to find by touch, and he soon turned it into a position where he could move the file back and forth comfortably. By rub-

bing a little butter along the cutting edge, he found
that the noise was scarcely audible—certainly too
slight to be heard on the first floor.

For the best part of an hour he worked, stealthily but with hardly a moment's rest. He could feel
the notch in the iron growing deeper. It must be
two-thirds of the way through, he thought. And
then catastrophe overtook him. He was just reaching for the piece of bread, to get more butter, when
suddenly it was snatched from under his hand.
The biggest rat he had ever seen had seized it and
scurried away across the floor.

Tad was more than startled. For a moment his
nerves were shaken, and he sat there trembling
with weariness and fright. Then the ridiculous side
of the situation struck him and he rocked back and
forth with smothered laughter. When the spasm
was over he tried to work on the fetter again and
found that the scraping of the dry file was becoming more and more noisy. Saliva would quiet it
for a stroke or two, but it dried too quickly. At
last he gave up the effort. He put the file away,
dropped the board back in place and curled up
exhausted in his corner, wishing desperately for
his snug blanket aboard the *Katy Roby*.

CHAPTER XIII

There may have been worse nights in history than the one Tad spent in that garret, but in all his experience he never was to know a longer or more nerve-racking one.

Rats scampered everywhere, in the walls and up and down the floor. He could hear them gnawing, squealing, fighting all about him.

Once or twice, when he drowsed off for a moment, their furry bodies brushed against his skin, waking him with a start. He had heard of rats attacking men in places like this. What if one of them should bite him there in the dark? He sat, tense and waiting, for hours on end, and shook his chain and thumped his hands on the floor to keep them away.

The lesser vermin in the rags about him were not so easily frightened off. He had discovered, almost as soon as he was put in the room, that Murrell's mention of fleas was more than idle chatter. Now, under cover of the darkness, they came in swarms to feast upon him. In a way, perhaps, they were a blessing, for they gave him little time to dwell on his graver troubles.

Nevertheless he was haunted all night by the thought of Abe's distress. What had the big flat-boatman thought of him when he failed to return at noon? Allen, doubtless, had stayed ashore drinking and enjoying himself, and Abe must have felt that Tad had betrayed his trust. At least so the boy pictured it to himself. Then he realized that the long-shanked Hoosier would be far more concerned with finding him than with blaming him. Just what would Abe do, he wondered. For he was positive that he would do something. Murrell and all his gang went armed to the teeth. If Abe should run afoul of some of them he would almost certainly be killed. Tad thought of the strong, homely, kindly face of his big friend and came near sobbing.

At last, toward dawn, he was too weary to fight the fleas, and hardly cared whether the rats bit him or not. Tumbled in a heap on the floor, he slept the sleep of sheer exhaustion.

The reflected light of a bright morning sun was in the room when he awoke. A clatter of pots and pans and an odor of cooking came up from below. Presently he heard boots thumping and the scrape of chairs and knew that the outlaws were sitting down to breakfast.

Rubbing his eyes, he looked about the dirty room

and saw that there was a little heap of iron filings on the floor where he had worked. Hastily he lifted the loose board and swept the tell-tale gray dust into the hole. He was none too soon, for a moment later he heard the pad of bare feet outside, and the sliding of the bolt on his door. Congo entered bearing his breakfast.

The meal this time was an unappetizing kind of corn-meal mush without milk. Tad had hoped to get some more butter. He hid his disappointment, however, and ate as much of the stuff as he could, knowing that he would need all his strength if he was ever to escape. There was also a cup of water which he drank eagerly.

When he had finished, Congo took the bowl and cup and paused in the doorway as before to grimace at him. This time the huge negro changed his gesture. With one hand he made the sign of a noose about his neck, winding up behind his left ear with a horrible jerk of the head and more silent laughter.

Tad, with a sick feeling at the pit of his stomach, wondered what other varieties of sudden death he would see illustrated before he left that filthy place.

The morning was well along—it must have been after ten o'clock, Tad thought—when there was a sound of heavy hoofs galloping up the road, and several riders dismounted in the yard. The boy could hear them swearing at the horses and then greeting Murrell and his companions as they approached the door.

These newcomers seemed to be members of the outlaw gang, for they spoke freely of Tad's capture and asked the chief what he planned to do with his prize. As they came into the room below, one of them was roaring with laughter. Tad took up the board in order to hear better and found he could make out nearly everything that was said.

"But the blankety-blankedest thing I ever saw, suh," one of the new men was remarking, "was this big Hoosier broadhorn steerer comin' up the Main Street. Seven foot if he was an inch—yes, suh, I'm not exaggeratin' a particle—seven foot tall! He marches up to the first saloon he sees and asks the bar-keep if he knows anything about a boy that's missin'. The man gives him some sort of a sassy answer, and next thing he knows this long-legged river hand has grabbed him by the neck and flung him out in the middle of the road.

"Fight? No, there was no fight. The Hoosier just goes along and leaves him there. At the next place the same thing happens, only the bartender saves his skin by apologizin' mighty quick when

he sees that long arm comin'. So it goes all the way
up the street.

"Finally he gets to Nolan's place. By this time
there's quite a crowd of flatboat and keel-boat men
followin' along to see the fun. An' drinkin' at Nolan's bar is some ark hand that pipes up and says
yes, indeed, he saw the boy. He was bein' carried
off by three men on horseback, ridin' hell-for-
leather up the South Bluff road.

" 'What did they look like?' asks Longshanks,
and the fellow tells him that the one holdin' the
boy was tall and rode a big sorrel horse with three
white stockin's.

"At that, half the river-men in the crowd shout
'Jack Murrell,' and there's a grand howdy-do.
The big Hoosier tries to find out where you'd be
likely to take the boy, but of course no one knows
a thing.

"I understand he's gone up to Natchez-on-the-
Hill this mornin', to try to raise a posse."

Tad heard Murrell's lazy laugh. "Huh," said
the leader, "he won't get far there. What say,
Carson, want to have a look at the youngster?"

There was a sound of boots that warned Tad
to put the board back in position. He crawled back
into the corner where the shadows were deepest

and turned the filed place in the fetter carefully under his ankle.

When the door opened he sat there sullen-faced, picking at the ragged edges of his shirt sleeve with listless fingers.

Murrell was accompanied by a big, florid young man in the dapper dress of a planter, who slapped the dust from his boots with a riding-whip as he stared down at the boy.

"Haw, haw! Fifty thousand—for that?" he laughed. "Here, step up, boy, and let's have a look at you!" And he flicked the stinging lash of his whip into the lad's neck. A sudden flush spread over Tad's face, but he sat perfectly still. Angrily, Carson threw up his arm for a full stroke, but Murrell detained him with a sharp word.

"Careful," he said. "He's mine, you know." For a moment Carson faced the cold gleam of the chief's eyes. Then his own eyes dropped. He gave an uneasy laugh and turned toward the stairs, and after another glance at Tad, Murrell followed him.

The time dragged by interminably. Buzzing flies made the daylight hours seem as unbearably long as the night had been. Sometime in the afternoon the boy dozed off and was finally awakened by the arrival of his supper. To his joy there was bread and butter. He was so hungry that there was a real temptation to gobble all of it, but he saved the last piece, pretending to eat it, as before.

Just as Congo stooped to pick up the plate, there came that ear-splitting whistle that Tad had heard once before, and the big negro leaped as if he had been shot. Without even a backward look he slipped through the door, fastened it, and hurried down the stairs.

Other horsemen had arrived, it seemed. Tad heard strange voices below, and after removing the board caught Murrell's answer.

"If they do come, it will be in daylight," he was saying. "We'll have to run him back to a safer place in the morning, and lie low for a few days."

The boy's heart sank. Tonight, it seemed, was his last chance. If he did not get away before morning he was to be taken off to some new stronghold where there would be even less hope of escape.

Quickly he took the file out of the hole and set to work. Before darkness had completely fallen he could see that another hour's labor would sever the broad iron ring. He rested a few minutes and then went on, pushing the file steadily back and forth. This time he took no chances with his bread and butter, but kept it tucked away in the bosom of his shirt.

From the noise in the room below he judged that there must be five or six men at least gathered about the table. They seemed to be playing cards and drinking, for he heard frequent orders for rum punch shouted at a servant they called Juba.

What game they were playing he could not tell, but the stakes must have been high. A loud voice, made thick by many potations, reached the boy distinctly through the garret floor,

"You goin' to stick along, Murrell?" the voice was saying. "You goin' to stick? Gettin' in pretty deep, ain't you? That's fifteen hundred you owe me now. All right, I'm raisin' it two hundred more. What d'ye say—want to put the boy up? Eh? That gilt-edged prisoner o' yours? I aim to back these cards all night; so you better unlimber some cash or else put up the boy."

Tad bent harder to his work, and the sweat streamed from his face as he filed. If they were making him a stake in their game and the cards went against Murrell, his new owner might come up at any moment to claim him. The file was almost through. He gave it a last stroke or two, and the fetter fell open with a sudden clank of metal.

Holding his breath, the boy waited to see if they

had heard, but it appeared that all in the lower room were too absorbed in what was going on there to notice any such trifling sound. With all possible care he lifted his ankle out of the broken clasp and stood up, feeling an exhilarating sense of freedom.

Cautiously, in the darkness, he moved across the room. The door was secured on the outside, as he had expected. He left it and turned toward the window, treading very softly and testing each board with his bare toes.

There had been a momentary lull in the voices downstairs. Now, with startling suddenness, some one ripped out an angry oath, and there was a commotion of chairs being pushed back. Two pistol shots rent the air, close together, and then all was quiet again except for a single low groan.

Tad stood still, trying to control the shaking of his knees.

"He's dead," came the heavy voice of Bull Whaley. "Well, we can't leave him here. Come, give me a hand, some one."

The house door opened and closed again, and then there was a short, ugly laugh, followed by a call for Juba and another round of drinks. Tad tiptoed forward to the window.

Where he had feared to find a complicated system of fastenings, there was only a big square nail driven part way into the frame above the lower sash. It was solidly imbedded in the wood, but by moving it up and down until it had a trifle of play, he was able at last to pull it out with his fingers.

To the boy's relief, the sash was loose enough to raise without too much effort. He lifted it an inch at a time, easing it past the squeaks, and braced it open with a two-foot length of stick which had been lying on the sill.

A young moon, partly obscured by clouds, shed a faint light over the dooryard. Tad could see the ground, fifteen feet below, with a tangled mass of rank weeds growing against the house. A score of yards beyond was the road, and then woods, black and dense, stretching away to the west. A little night breeze came in the window with refreshing coolness.

Tad stood there for a while, wondering what time of night it was and how late it would be before the outlaws went to sleep. He was afraid they might stay a long time over their liquor. Climbing down past the window of the room in which they sat seemed a foolhardy plan, but Tad grew restless at the thought of a long wait.

At last he decided to go back to his hole in the floor and listen to their talk. Treading lightly but swiftly, he retraced his steps. The garret was as dark as pitch, but he believed he knew his way. He must be nearing the place now. And even as this thought crossed his mind he stepped directly into the opening. There was a crackle of breaking lath and a crash of plaster, and Tad's foot went through the ceiling of the room beneath. He withdrew it instantly and stood there trembling, his heart pounding with terror and with fury at his own clumsiness.

A sound of startled swearing came from below, and through the aperture he caught a glimpse of flushed faces staring upward. For a long moment they stood so. Then the faces disappeared and there was a rush of feet through the hallway leading to the stairs.

Only one course lay open for Tad, and he took it. Darting across the garret, he scrambled through the window and let himself down, his hands gripping the sill, till his feet touched the ledge above the ground floor window. Would they see him? He had no way of telling how many had stayed in the room below. But he could already hear shouts at the top of the stairs, and some one was fumbling at the bolt.

With a deep intake of breath the boy let go one hand, swung outward and jumped.

CHAPTER XIV

THE TEN-FOOT DROP to the ground jarred Tad from head to toe but did not really hurt him. He was up in an instant, and without even a backward glance at the house he made for the trees across the road. As he started to run he tripped over something bulky in the grass and saw with a shudder that it was the body of the man called Carson, still and cold, a ray of moonlight falling on his white, upturned face. Tad sped onward, cleared the road in a long leap, in order to leave no track in the dust, and plunged into the brush on the farther side. The dark wall of leaves closed behind him, and he knew that for the moment at least he was beyond the outlaws' reach, but he did not slacken speed. Tumbling over fallen logs, diving headforemost through thickets, dashing forward wherever an opening showed between the tree trunks, he kept on. Weak as he was from scanty food and lack of sleep, he must have traveled a good half mile through the woods before he fell, too exhausted to pick himself up.

For a long time he lay there, panting, till the vast ache inside his ribs grew less painful and finally departed. Then at last he rose on wobbly legs and went forward. When he was a prisoner in the outlaws' garret he had made no definite plans beyond escaping from the house. But now he saw quite clearly that some sort of intelligent planning would be necessary if he wanted to avoid getting lost or recaptured.

To reach the river was his first problem. If he could strike the bank he was sure he could find Natchez, somewhere a few miles to the north. So he went on, searching for a more open space where he might get his bearings.

For what seemed like an age he plowed through dense timber, where he could see only an occasional gleam of moonlight, much less a recognizable star. But finally the trees opened out in front of him and he found himself in the edge of a small clearing, full of stumps and brush, but giving a clear view overhead. A few clouds still covered part of the sky, but he made out the Dipper, and following the two pointers, located the North Star. It was ahead of him and a little to the right, so that he knew his general direction had been good. What he wanted now was to bear toward the left, shaping a westerly course, and so reach the river bluffs.

At the farther side of the clearing he struck

into what seemed to be a wood path leading westward. Rough as it was, he found he could walk along it with much less difficulty than through the trackless brush, and as long as it continued fairly straight he had no fear of losing his direction.

For more than a mile he followed this trail, and came at length to a narrow little valley where the path led off to the right along the brink of the ravine. As he paused, undecided, a faint sound of water came to him from somewhere below in the undergrowth. He had been desperately thirsty for hours. In a moment he had scrambled down the bank and was bending above a shallow little stream. Down he went on hands and knees and drank his fill of the clear, cold water. And then, just as he was getting to his feet, there came a sound that fairly froze his heart with fear. Still far off, it was, but unmistakable—the deep, bell-like baying of a hound.

Until that moment Tad had not thought of dogs. Yet it was natural enough that Murrell should have them. In his trade of slave-stealing, he must often find use for bloodhounds.

The muffled note rang out again. Was it nearer this time? On his trail—*his* trail! They were after him with dogs! For an instant Tad felt the panic terror that makes the hunted rabbit run in circles.

His only impulse was to rush off blindly, somewhere—anywhere.

Then some measure of sense returned to him and he began thinking, swiftly. Up to that point the scent would be fresh and strong, easily followed. His pursuers would make far better time than he had made, thrashing through the brush. From now on he must baffle them, or he was lost.

The stream was hardly more than a rivulet, a few feet wide, but it offered him his only chance to cover his scent. Plunging in, he found it less than knee-deep, with a fairly smooth, sandy bottom. He followed it downstream, wading fast, and keeping an eye on the direction it was taking, when the leaves overhead permitted a view of the stars.

Once or twice he had to climb out to get around fallen trees, and this gave him an idea. Wherever there was a likely opening on either bank, leading away from the stream, he left the water, ran a few steps into the woods and returned, as nearly as possible in the same tracks. Then he waded on with all the speed he could muster.

Occasionally the wind bore to him the cry of the hound, sometimes clearer, sometimes fainter, but always a sound that chilled his blood.

Tad had long since passed the winded stage. He went on steadily, his breathing a succession of gasps that no longer seemed to hurt, a deadness in his legs and a queer ringing in his ears. He had no idea how long he had been running so, when suddenly the brook deepened and his numbed senses were shocked wide awake by a plunge into cold water.

He realized, as he floundered up again, that the sky overhead was open. He was standing up to his neck in a broad marshy pool that stretched away to left and right for a long distance. Under the ghostly moon it lay dark and mysterious, wholly silent except for the muffled plash of a heron hunting frogs. Like every boy, Tad had a horror of swimming in strange water at night. He stood there, shivering, trying to make up his mind. The opposite bank was not so far away, but sluggish ponds . . . water moccasins . . .

The bay of the bloodhound came to him again, unexpectedly close this time. He waited no longer but threw himself forward, swimming with all his might. The pool was only thirty or forty yards across at this place, and in a few strokes he was halfway over. Then a vicious cramp caught at the big muscles in the back of his thigh—twisting him with pain till he almost went under. He managed to straighten the leg and struggled on, kicking only with the other, till he felt ooze under his toes, and crawled out somehow through slimy reeds and lily-pads to the soft black earth of the bank.

There for a while he lay, his exhaustion so complete that he scarcely cared what happened. Both his legs were cruelly knotted with cramps, and his whole body ached with weariness. Rest he must have if he were ever to reach the river. He crept a little farther into the reeds and lay on his back, staring up at the stars and listening to the intermittent baying of the hound.

At last the cramps left him and he thought he had recovered his wind sufficiently to go on. But just as he was rising to his knees there came a thrashing in the underbrush near the mouth of the brook and he heard men's voices. A light breeze was blowing across the pond from them to him so that he caught some of the words plainly.

"What's the matter with ol' Red-eye—lost the scent again?" came Bull Whaley's panting bass. And as if in answer the bloodhound spoke—a full-throated, menacing challenge that fairly lifted the hair on Tad's head. Through the screening reeds he could see the beast on the other side of the pool, gray and gigantic in the moonlight, its long ears trailing the ground as it nosed here and there along the bank.

Behind, in the shadow, was the broad, squat

HE COULD SEE THE BEAST ON THE OTHER SIDE OF
THE POOL

figure of Whaley, and another man whom Tad did not recognize was holding the hound's leash.

A stream of profanity came from this second man. "Lost him!" he growled. "Must have swum across. What d'ye say—want to send the dog over?"

"No use," returned the other. "The boy's most likely a long ways off by now. An' even if Red-eye got over without bein' bit by a snake, I wouldn't foller him. The nearest place to cross is Cordle's Bridge, a mile away. What I say is we'd best git back to the horses an' make it down to the river road in a hurry. We'd ought to head him off there, sure."

They stood there arguing for a while, then turned back into the woods, dragging the huge, unwilling hound. And Tad, feeling that he had at least a momentary respite from pursuit, started toward the setting moon once more.

The rest had helped both his legs and his courage. Now that he knew how the outlaws expected to capture him, he believed he had a chance to outwit them, while if he had not overheard their plans, he might have walked straight into their ambush on the river road.

The shore of the pond was fringed with a sparse growth of saplings and brush, through which Tad made his way without much difficulty. Beyond it he could catch glimpses of a broad open space, gleaming palely in the moonlight. At first he thought it was water—a larger pond, perhaps—and his heart sank at the idea of having to swim again. But when he reached the edge of the trees he saw that what lay before him was a great cotton field, white with opening bloom. Easily half a mile wide, it stretched back to the north and east so far that his eyes lost it in the moonlit haze.

Crossing the waist-high cotton was dangerous, Tad knew. He veered to the left, skirting the end of the field, and at its farther corner came on a well-defined path leading into the woods. It bore a little north of west, in the direction he wished to follow, and he could see from the grass and brush in the track that it was little used. After a careful scrutiny of the cotton field for pursuers, he went forward along the path as fast as his weary legs would carry him.

Once the whir of a rattler, behind him, made cold chills run down his spine and gave speed to his feet. And half a mile farther on he was frightened almost out of his wits when a partly-grown razor-back boar leaped up, grunting, from its bed beside the path, and dashed off into the woods.

When the moon set, Tad had no choice but to

stay where he was and rest. He tried to feel his way along in the inky dark, but after he had stumbled against trees and nearly lost the path, he gave it up. There were still two or three hours till dawn, and he was very tired. A few yards off the path he found a place where he could sit, with his back against a tree. And in thirty seconds he was asleep.

Fortunately the cramped position he was in woke him before daylight and he staggered up, stiff and sore, but with his strength renewed. A faint grayness was beginning to show through the trees, so that now he had no trouble in following the path. He had a feeling that the river could not be far off.

A moment later the cheerful blast of a steamboat whistle sounded, close at hand. Tad's heart pounded with joy, and he pushed forward almost at a run. Within a hundred yards he came to a place where he could glimpse the road, brown and dusty in the increasing light, bending south along the crest of the bluff.

He abandoned the path and cut into the brush, striking northward with the highway and the river below on his left. He was looking for a good place to cross the road and make the descent of the bluff. Just as he thought he had found such a spot, and was preparing to leave the shelter of the undergrowth, his ears caught a faint clink of metal. He crouched where he was, waiting. Soon the sound was repeated, and with it he heard the musical jingle of a bridle chain. Then came a man's voice, muffled, quieting a restless horse, and a moment later he heard the soft thud of hoofs on grass.

Three mounted men came down the road from Natchez, riding silently in single file, their lathered horses at a walk. They were wrapped in cloaks and their hats were pulled low over their faces, but Tad knew them. The leader rode a big sorrel with three white legs.

Almost opposite Tad they pulled up and talked in low tones for a minute. He could not hear their words, but their gestures were short and angry. Hunched there in their saddles, they looked like ruffled birds of prey.

The leader jerked his horse around, motioned to one of the riders to stay where he was, and with the other at his heels, set off down the road. The man who remained looked after them grouchily for a moment, then swung down from his horse, pulled the reins over his arm, and sat down with his back against a stump.

As quietly as he knew how, Tad crawled back a

dozen yards or more into the woods. When he was
sure the rank growth screened him completely, he
got up and started northward again, fairly holding his breath in his effort to make no noise.

After a while he knew he was out of earshot of
the watcher by the road and could move faster.
The sun rose, bringing beauty to the woods. He
heard negroes singing, and soon a big mule-cart
creaked by, with half a dozen plantation hands on
their way to the fields, and a white overseer riding
abreast. Birds made a background of music for
all the other sounds of the waking day.

Tad passed a bend in the road and worked himself down into the bushes that fringed the ditch
beside it. He looked long and listened carefully in
both directions. Then with his heart in his mouth,
he made the dash for the opposite side. Three seconds, and it was done. The brush whipped shut
behind him. He waited a little to see if any one was
in pursuit, then turned and pushed his way
through the tangle of vines and creepers that
crowned the edge of the bluff.

There, a hundred feet and more below, was the
vast, muddy tide of the river that had made him
feel so lonely and depressed three short weeks ago.
How he welcomed it now! Spread out in a great
sunlit panorama, he saw the little arks and keel-

boats go gliding down, no bigger than chips on the yellow flood. And those tiny black figures, like ants, that worked at the sweeps or sat about the breakfast fires—those were his friends. He belonged to their brotherhood now. Old Trader Magoon and the jolly red-bearded captain from St. Louis, big, brave, awkward, kind-hearted Abe, and even Allen, with his human failings—they would all fight for him.

Something like a sob rose in his throat, and he had to choke it back. What was the matter with him anyway? It must be hunger. He remembered that he hadn't eaten much for two days. Well, it was time he was moving.

With another look around, to make sure no one watched him from the road, he started scrambling down the face of the bluff.

CHAPTER XV

As he descended, Tad could see the levee, below, and half a mile to the northward the huddled houses of Natchez-under-the-Hill. There was the big steamboat landing, piled with freight, and beyond it the swarming flatboat fleet, so close, now, that he almost fancied he could pick out the little *Katy Roby* at her moorings.

Clinging by roots and creepers, sliding from one grass tuft to the next, the boy went swiftly down. At the foot of the steep slope was a narrow marshy tract hemmed in by the levee. There was no road except the footway along the levee top, but a few shanties were scattered here and there—the cabins of free negroes, Tad thought—and among the evil-looking pools of green water, paths ran from one clump of great mossy live oaks to the next. He followed one of these, skirting a stagnant pond where the whole surface was covered with a weedy scum. An alligator moved lazily, thrusting up its long snout within a yard of Tad's heel, and great swarms of mosquitoes rose on all sides to meet him. He broke into a run.

Beyond the first clump of trees he passed the door of a squalid shack where dogs yapped at his heels and a frightened black woman wrapped her skirts about a child that screamed when it saw him. After he had driven the curs away with a stick, he went on more slowly. The morning was growing hot, and a desperate thirst possessed him. He thought of stopping at one of the negro cabins and asking for a drink, but the sight of the unspeakable filth around them decided him against it. After all, he was almost there. He could stand another ten minutes.

As he neared the town, the path ran through a dense clump of scrub willows that reached from the levee almost back to the foot of the bluff. Tad prudently slipped into this willow thicket as he drew close to the landing, and squirmed forward till he could command a view of the big dock, the street, and the flatboats beyond. His first glance told him it was lucky he had reconnoitered. For in addition to the handful of negroes who were rolling bales and barrels in the sleepy sunshine, he saw three horses tied to the rail before a corner tavern, and three men with hats pulled low over their faces, lounging in the shadows. One sat on the tavern veranda, watching the street. One patrolled the landing in leisurely fashion. And one stood idly under a tree with his eye on the movements of the flatboatmen.

If Murrell was one of them—and Tad thought the tall figure on the landing was he—he had changed horses since daybreak. The famous three-stocking sorrel was not among the mounts at the hitching-rail.

All this was a blow to Tad's hopes. Where he had expected to reach the haven of the *Katy Roby* in another moment or two, he saw that he might now have to wait for hours. His thirst was becoming almost unbearable. The whole inside of his mouth and his tongue felt parched and swollen. Mosquitoes in myriads came to sing their shrill refrain around his head, and other pests, he knew, would soon discover his hiding-place.

At last he could stand the torture of sitting still no longer. He got to his feet, peering through the willow branches. There, not a hundred yards away, he could see Allen standing on the forward deck of the flatboat, smoking his pipe and looking up the town's main street as if he were waiting for some one.

If only he could signal him in some way! But there were the three grim watchers—desperate men, as Tad knew—who would not hesitate to use their pistols with a fifty-thousand-dollar prize in sight. It might cost his friends their lives if he showed himself.

He had thought of swimming under the landing, but there would still be a sixty-foot stretch of water to cross under the hawk eyes of that tall man, slouching in the shade of a pile of boxes. Still, he reflected, he could hardly be worse off in the water than dying a slow death by thirst and mosquitoes here.

Very quietly he made his way through the willows to the levee. The piling of the dock rose close by—almost close enough to touch. On his stomach, he crawled over the top of the embankment and slid like a muskrat into the yellow water beyond. In a few quick strokes he was under the landing and hidden from view.

He held on to one of the big cypress piles and gulped a swallow or two of river water to take the edge off his thirst. Then he made his way forward under the shadowy planking of the wharf.

Suddenly there was a shout, somewhere above, and a pounding of many feet that went by over his head, shaking dust down through the cracks. He stayed where he was, his heart beating fast. Then there came the loud blast of a steamboat whistle, and he understood the reason for the stampede.

Alternately swimming and stopping to listen, he made his way to the outer end of the wharf.

There, holding to one of the great clumps of mooring piles, he watched the slim white prow of the pride of the river—the *Natchez* herself—come sweeping in to the landing. With a swiftness at which he marveled, the great paddles swung her into position, and amid the shouts of deck hands he heard the heavy cable drop with a crash on the planks over his head. In another moment the big steamer was moored, side-on to the wharf, and the gangplanks were run out. The steady rumble of loading began.

From where Tad was he could see forward under the broad overhanging deck of the *Natchez* to the low patch of daylight at her bows. And as he looked, an idea came to him. He remembered how the forward end of the *Tecumseh*, jutting well beyond the landing, had seemed to be almost within arm's reach of the flatboat, that first morning in Natchez. Under the shelter of the steamer, he could get many feet closer to his goal without being seen.

He let go of the post to which he had been holding, and swam out under the boat's deck. It was like being in a long, low-roofed, watery tunnel. The deck was only two or three feet above the level of the river and was built out from the hull a good ten feet. It was shored up by a row of diagonal braces, and to these Tad clung, pulling himself slowly along. When he reached the end of the wharf he could see that his hopes were at least partly justified. The steamer's prow extended at least thirty feet nearer to the moored flatboats, and he was certain that for the best part of that distance he would be well hidden from eyes on the landing.

Keeping as far as possible under the projecting shelf, he pulled himself forward by the bracing timbers. Finally he came to a point where the deck narrowed rapidly toward the bow and no longer afforded any cover. As nearly as he could judge, about fifteen yards still separated him from the *Katy Roby*. He was close enough to see every homely plank and seam of the little craft, even to the familiar marks of Abe's mighty ax on the hewn corner posts.

A sudden fear seized him now—a fear that Abe or Allen might appear at the gunwale and see him. That would be dangerous, he knew.

Obviously, he could not stay where he was. Something had to be done, and done at once. With desperation in his heart, the boy again measured the distance to the flatboat, then drew a deep breath, and took off from the steamer's side in a long plunge. He had swum under water many times before, but never when he was so tired, or with so much at stake.

Five strokes he took—ten—twelve, with his lungs ready to burst for air—thirteen—fourteen—fifteen—sixteen—he *must* come up—seventeen—eighteen, and his hand touched planks! He was there, safe under the flatboat's counter. For a moment he lay with mouth and nose just out of water, gasping in the breaths he so sorely needed. A stray end of rope, hanging from the stern, gave him something to hold on to.

From the tall, white *Natchez* there came a jangle of bells and a thrashing of the water as her paddles turned over. This was Tad's chance. All eyes would be on the steamer for the next minute or two. He took a firm grip on the rope and went up with a kick of his feet. At the gunwale he had just strength enough left to fling up a leg and pull himself over. Five seconds later he rolled over the edge of the after deck and dropped without ceremony into the middle of Allen's preparations for dinner.

If Tad had not instantly signaled him to silence it is certain that the *Katy Roby's* cook would have yelled aloud in terror. As it was he toppled over backward on the planking and sat there looking comically pale.

"Great—hallelujah—fishhooks!" he choked out, at last. "I shore never looked to see your face ag'in, boy! How in Tarnation did ye git away?"

"I'll tell you—pretty soon," grinned Tad, still too weary to talk. "Where's Abe?"

"Up thar in the town—Natchez-'top-o'-the-Hill," said Allen. "He's been tryin' to git 'em to send a sheriff's posse arter you. But gosh, boy, look at them feet!"

Tad was bleeding from half a dozen cuts and bruises that he had got in the course of his flight. Until now he had not even noticed them. His shirt was in tatters, and even the stout homespun trousers, in addition to being heavy with mud and water, had been torn in several places. Gaunt with hunger and fatigue and wet as a drowned kitten, he looked little like his usual sturdy self.

But Poke knew him. The gangling baby bear stretched his chain as far as it would go and licked with a warm pink tongue at Tad's face. Chuckling with delight, the boy rolled over to scratch his pet's inquisitive round ears. And at that moment a long shadow fell across the deck and they heard the tread of moccasined feet.

Abe, still frowning and preoccupied with the business that had taken him ashore, dropped down from the fore deck and almost stepped on Tad before he saw him.

"Wal, I'll be—" he began. But his vocabulary, for once, was totally inadequate to the occasion.

"Quick, Abe!" Tad implored him. "Get down here out of sight, if you're going to look like that. There's three of Murrell's men watching on the landing."

The big Hoosier crouched obediently, but Allen started up with an oath. "Whar's that gun o' mine?" he asked in a belligerent tone.

"Hold on," said Abe. "Don't be a dum fool, Allen. This is no time to git mixed up in a fight. Now we've got Tad back, our job is to take him out o' here safe. Let's see, now—Tad, you'd best crawl in under the edge o' that tarpaulin, jest in case o' trouble.

"Allen, you act unconcerned-like, an' go on gittin' some dinner together. I'm goin' to shove off. Wait, now, till I git to lookin' glum ag'in."

With a comical effort, he twisted his gaunt face into a heavy frown.

"That ought to fool 'em," he muttered, and stood up, with a dejected stoop to his shoulders. Slowly he mounted the forward deck, swung over in a long stride to the next craft, and so reached the mooring-stakes along the levee. As he cast off the rope and proceeded slowly to coil it over his arm, a keel-boat man hailed him, three or four boats away.

"What's up, Longshanks? Gwine to leave without the youngster?" he asked.

Abe shrugged his shoulders. "'Tain't no use to try any more," he replied, gloomily. "They're all afraid to move, up in the town. I reckon we might better be gittin' our cargo to market."

"Yeah," agreed the other, and spat over the rail. "It's tough luck, though. 'Good-by, five thousand dollars,' eh?"

An angry blaze lit Abe's gray eyes. He started to speak, then changed his mind. Dropping the coil of rope on the fore deck, he picked up one of the rowing-sweeps and planted it on firm bottom. Then with a heave of his mighty shoulders, he drove the *Katy Roby* straight out from the levee.

As the current caught them they were swung close to the corner piles of the wharf. Abe put his oars in the chocks and began rowing, strongly but without haste.

"Keep hid, now," came Allen's whisper. "Thar's a feller watchin' us up thar on the landin'. Big, tall feller with his hat over his eyes.

'Pears like he's mighty interested in what we've got aboard.''

''Wal,'' he called out derisively, ''think ye'll be able to reco'nize us next time?''

There was no answer from the man on the wharf.

''Allen,'' said Tad, when they had dropped the landing well astern, ''do you know who that was you hailed? I do. It was Jack Murrell.''

Allen's face went pale. ''No-o!'' he said, in an awe-stricken whisper. ''You don't tell me—*Murrell!*''

''He'll recognize you, all right,'' Tad could not help chuckling. ''He never forgets a face.''

But as the boy rose from his place under the tarpaulin and looked astern, he wondered if perhaps his jest had been ill-timed. At the hitching-rail in front of the water-front saloon he could see three men mounting their horses. They turned, in a swirl of dust, as he watched, and spurred away up the town's main street toward the bluff. And wherever they were going, they evidently meant business.

CHAPTER XVI

TAD KEPT his misgivings to himself as the flatboat voyaged southward. Both of his companions were so genuinely happy over his safe return that nothing else really seemed to matter. They fed him and pampered him, dried and mended his clothes, and treated him in general like a long-lost brother.

Tad responded with a full heart. He ate the feast of corn bread, bacon, and coffee that Allen prepared, and had no need to feign an appetite. And to the delighted ears of his companions he unfolded, bit by bit, as his strength returned, the tale of his capture and escape.

When he described how he first happened to run afoul of the outlaws he saw Allen redden uneasily, and the baleful glance that Abe turned on the son of his employer told Tad how deeply the matter must have been discussed.

He went on to tell of the ride, of the lonely house in the woods, and of the great black deaf-mute who was Murrell's servant.

"I've heard o' him," put in Allen, his eyes wide

with excitement. ''Some ark hand from up the Yazoo said he'd done caught a sight of him once. Most o' the keel-boat men, though, say they're sartin he ain't no nigger at all, but some sort of a gorilla.''

Tad did not laugh. The horror of those silent visits that Congo had paid him was still too fresh in his memory.

''No,'' he answered. ''He's a man, all right. But, gosh! I believe I'd *rather* have a gorilla after me than that big black devil. Ugh!'' And he shivered a little in spite of the noonday heat.

He told them of the arrival of the strangers at the house, and how he had heard their talk of the doings in Natchez.

''That's what I was afeared of,'' said Abe, with a nod. ''Every move I made in the town, I had a feelin' there were spies a-watchin'. I was sure that if we did git a posse together, they'd have wind of it long 'fore we got thar. An' added to that, all the head folks in Natchez were either scairt o' Murrell or else in cahoots with him. I didn't rightly know whar to turn next.''

The tall lad's voice grew gruff, and he shook his head as he looked at Tad. ''That shorely was a mean two days,'' he said.

''All over now, though,'' replied the boy, with

an understanding grin. And he went on with the recounting of his adventures.

Some time past the middle of the afternoon they were running eastward on the outer edge of a great ox-bow bend where the strong current bit deep into the Mississippi side. Floating swiftly as they were, with the bank only sixty or seventy yards away, Abe was rowing, and Allen was at the steering-sweep watching for possible snags. Suddenly Abe pointed at the top of the bluff, high above them and a little distance upstream.

"Look a' thar!" he exclaimed. "They're out o' sight now, but you'll see 'em in a jiffy past that clump o' trees."

Tad watched with all his eyes, and even Allen turned to look where the big fellow was pointing. But the seconds passed and nothing happened.

"Ye'd ought to have a sunshade," the steersman remarked solicitously. "This heat's makin' ye see things."

Abe frowned in puzzlement. "It beats me," he said. "I'd ha' sworn I saw three men on horseback, gallopin' along that road on the bluff. What the 'Nation do ye s'pose become of 'em?"

"Probably thought that long arm o' your'n was a gun aimed at 'em," Allen suggested. But Tad was less inclined to take the incident as a joke.

He approved Abe's judgment that evening when the lanky oarsman pulled over toward the western shore.

"I sort o' feel the need of a change o' climate," was Abe's comment. "Reckon we'll find the night air a bit healthier over here in Louisiana."

Weary as he was, Tad fell asleep ten minutes after supper was over and never opened his eyes again until the smoke from the breakfast fire blew into them next morning. But he knew without being told that his two friends had stood guard by turns, all night.

"With a good start this mornin'," said Abe, cocking an eye at the rising sun, "we'd ought to be 'most a hundred mile from Natchez by nightfall. I reckon we made thirty-five yesterday. Suits me to git as far away from that 'ar town as we kin —an' as fast."

The rest of the crew being in complete agreement with this idea, they finished breakfast in a hurry and were soon spinning downstream again. By noon they had put another thirty miles between them and the scene of Tad's capture, and all of them began to breathe easier. But in his desire to add to the *Katy Roby's* speed, Abe pulled a trifle too hard on one of the forward sweeps, and the deeply-worn handle broke with a snap.

There was nothing to do but land and make a new one. Abe took the stern oar and swung over to the Louisiana bank. After they had tied up it took the two flatboatmen the best part of an hour to find the kind of tree they liked in this unfamiliar, half-tropical forest. When at last they had chosen a good-sized sapling, Abe whetted his ax and hewed swiftly away, first shaping a blade at the butt of the log, then cutting a long, rough handle out of the straight-grained center. Finally, with his clasp knife, he smoothed up the inequalities along the shaft, and before sunset they had a new oar as good as the old one.

Tad, looking out across the river while the others worked, saw what he took at first for a log drifting down rapidly along the Mississippi side. It was not until he caught the flash of a paddle that he realized it was not a log but a dugout canoe. Once, when the little craft was silhouetted for a moment against a lighter background, he made out a single dark figure paddling strongly in the stern. The next instant the canoe vanished past the end of an island.

If Tad had not been nervously keyed up by what he had been through, it is probable he would hardly have noticed the occurrence. Canoes were not very common along the lower river, but he

had seen them occasionally, manned by Indians or
white trappers, coming down from the smaller
streams.

It was not the craft itself but something swift
and furtive in the motions of the paddler that gave
the boy an odd feeling of uneasiness. However, he
did not even mention the canoe to Abe and Allen,
for he was a little ashamed of his vague fears.

When the oar was finished they pushed on for
another hour or two, and Abe was in favor of
making up the time they had lost by traveling part
of the night. But the sky, which had been clear
most of the afternoon, had started to cloud up at
sunset and was now heavily overcast.

"She'll be black as yer hat in another hour,"
Allen counseled. "With no moon to help, ye'll
never be able to steer betwixt all these islands."

"All right," Abe agreed grudgingly. "But we'll
have to make it watch an' watch ag'in tonight, if
we tie up here."

Though Allen could see little sense in this pre-
caution, he finally consented, provided he could
take the first turn, and they made their mooring
for the night. Tad offered to stand one guard, but
the others would not hear of it. Probably he would
have made a poor watchman, for as it turned out
he slept again like a log from dark to daylight.

"What d'ye say *now?*" Allen called cheerfully from the breakfast fire next morning. "Not a sound all night. We jest wasted four hours o' sleep apiece."

But Abe, who had gone ashore for more wood, did not reply. He was stooping over something on the ground, examining it intently.

"Come here a minute," he said, finally, and both the others went to join him, sensing a discovery of some kind.

His face wore a curious expression when he looked up. "If I was a real crackajack at this sort o' thing," he said, "I'd tell ye jest when this yere was made, an' by what. The way things are, I kin only guess."

He was kneeling before a little bare patch of black earth. At first Tad thought there was nothing there. Then he got down beside Abe, and when he peered closely he saw, very faint across the firm surface, the print of a naked foot.

Allen whistled softly. "Big b'ar, ain't it?" he asked.

"Look again," said Abe, laconically.

The track was long and immensely broad, and the impressions of all five toes were visible at the end farthest from the river. But Tad, even with his slight knowledge of woodcraft, knew that a bear

HE SAW THE PRINT OF A NAKED FOOT

track would show the claw-points beyond the toes.

"It's a man, isn't it?" he said, almost in a whisper.

"If it's a man," Abe answered slowly, "he's got the biggest foot I ever hope to see. It's as long as mine, an' most half ag'in as wide. What's more, I should say he'd never had a pair o' shoes on in his life. Look at them splay toes."

Tad saw that the print of the great toe was separated by a full inch from that of the second.

"Who—who do you think made it?" he asked.

Abe considered a moment. "I think it was a nigger," he said. "Most likely a runaway slave, but anyhow a mighty big feller—one o' the biggest. What I really want to know, though, is when he come by here. If 'twas last night it must ha' been in the first few hours, 'cause—"

"No, sirree!" Allen spoke up indignantly. "Everything was quiet 'round yere in *my watch* —outside o' the noise you made snorin'."

Abe grinned. "Wal," said he, "thar's no way I know of to settle it. An' he didn't do us much harm that I can see. The sensible thing fer us to do is head south an' leave him."

With a last look at the mysterious footprint, they boarded the *Katy Roby* once more and shoved out into the current, eating breakfast as they went.

"Anyhow," said Allen, casting a sidelong look at the landing-place, "he was headed away from us when he made that track." He took a mouthful of bacon, and then—"I hope he keeps on goin'," he chuckled.

None of them felt very talkative that morning. They took their turns at the oars and tiller and kept the flatboat moving at her best speed, which now averaged four to five miles an hour. The current was perceptibly slower as they went farther south, and the channel seemed deeper, with fewer sand-bars. There were numerous jungle-clad islands, however, and in some of the narrow cuts through which they passed, the giant creepers and the long festoons of Spanish moss came trailing across the deck with a cool, slithery sound.

At noon they came into the head of a long open reach, and Abe stopped rowing to mop his sun-burned forehead.

"Whew!" he breathed. "Hotter'n corn-hoein' time up home. It takes somethin' to make me sweat, too. Wal, we don't have to work so hard from now on. Let's see—" he did some counting on his fingers—"we must be 'most a hundred an' ten mile below Natchez right now. We'll be down to Baton Rouge 'fore night, an' I'm told thar's good landin's all along the Sugar Coast, below thar."

They had left the region of pine forest behind them now and had come fairly into the heart of old Louisiana. On both sides of the river were the great Creole plantations with their stately white houses and stately French names. Sometimes when the flatboat ran close inshore, they caught intimate glimpses of lovely formal gardens and verandas gay with laughing girls.

Allen, staring open-mouthed at these creatures of a different world, turned to Abe at length with a wag of the head.

"By the ol' jumpin' sassafras," he said, "I b'lieve Tad was tellin' us the truth 'bout wearin' shoes, back east. Did ye see them two women-folks jes' now? White stockin's *an'* slippers on, right in the heat o' the summer!"

They went past the town of Baton Rouge, late that afternoon. Tad remembered, as he saw the landing and the stores, that his letter to his father had never been sent, and asked if he might land.

"Sure ye kin," said Abe. "But we'll be in New Orleans ourselves in another two days—maybe as quick as the mail. Why not wait an' surprise yer Pappy, now?"

This suggestion met a ready response from Tad. He could picture that meeting very clearly, and although he would not postpone his father's happiness even by a day if he could avoid it, the idea of a surprise appealed to him.

They came, in the falling dusk, to a low wooden landing-stage built out from the levee. There was no house in sight except a long, roofed storage shed with a few empty molasses barrels piled beneath it, but a white-painted sign bore the inscription, "La Plantation de Madame Duquesne."

Abe ran the broadhorn in alongside the dock and made fast to a post.

"Couldn't ask fer a snugger place to tie up than this, could ye?" he asked. "Tad, you run up thar in the cane a ways, an' cut us some sugar sticks to chaw. Allen an' I'll git the wood an' water an' start supper."

Taking the short hand-ax, the boy followed the top of the levee for a little distance and turned in along a raised wagon-track that led back into the tall cane. He went on till he found some pieces that suited him, cut half a dozen lengths with the ax, and shouldering the bundle, started back toward the river.

He had almost reached the levee when there was a sudden movement in the thicket behind him, a crashing of the cane and a sound like the thud of feet.

Tad did not even wait to glance over his shoulder but made a leap for the levee and ran along it toward the boat with all his might. When he got to the landing he looked back. There was no sign nor sound of a pursuer. The peaceful calm of evening lay over the river and the shore.

"Who were ye racin' with?" asked Allen jocosely.

Tad recovered his breath and told them in a few words what he had heard. His face was still pale, and he felt a trifle shaky, but he tried to laugh it off.

"I guess it was nothing to be afraid of," he said. "Maybe it was a cow."

"Or a rabbit," said Allen. "They make a mighty loud noise sometimes, in the woods."

Abe shook his head. "Sounds more like a b'ar, to me," he put in. "Or it might even be a panther. At any rate it wouldn't do a mite o' harm to have a fire on the levee tonight. That'd keep the skeeters away as well as the varmints."

They gathered more wood, and after supper built a slow-burning fire of half-green chunks on the levee, close to where the boat was moored.

Tad gave Poke a piece of sugar cane to worry, and watched the delighted little bear suck the sweetness out of the stick as if it had been a bottle. They all chewed on the succulent joints of cane till the dark had settled over the river. Then with the usual good-nights they spread their blankets and turned in.

"It's hot tonight," Abe yawned. "I'm goin' to give you boys more room." And so saying, he took his bed up to the raised deck forward.

In two minutes everything was quiet, aboard. But Tad did not sleep. He was thinking of the footprint they had found that morning, and of the noise in the cane. In spite of all the reassuring things he could tell himself, the thought persisted in his mind that it was not a cow he had heard—nor a bear—nor even a panther. It was a man.

CHAPTER XVII

Sleep overcame Tad at last, but when it did it was a strange, restless slumber, full of dreams.

He seemed to be running, leaden-footed, down the bed of an interminable brook, where at every step the deep, black mud sucked horribly at his heels. He struggled forward, his heart almost bursting with effort, and always behind him he could hear the fierce, wild baying of dogs.

The black swamp grew firmer about him, and there in the surface of the mud he saw a huge track, broad, misshapen, with a great toe that looked half like a thumb. And suddenly the cry of the hounds ended in a whimper, and he was fleeing from a pack of huge black stooping shapes that ran through the woods on their hind legs—more silent—more terrible than dogs.

He rushed on, stumbled, tried to get up, and found that all the strength had run out of his body. His pursuers were close upon him now, enormous in the dark, their long arms stretched to seize him. He tried to cry out, but no sound would come from his throat. Then through the fringes of his dream he heard Poke give a frightened squeal that turned into a growl, and there was a low, startled oath somewhere close by. And suddenly Tad found himself awake.

He was sitting upright on his blanket in the flatboat, clutching what he realized was the handle of the ax. Above him, black against the red glow of the fire, loomed a vast ape-like figure, and there were half a dozen others moving on the levee and in the boat. He found his voice, then.

"Abe—Allen!" he screamed, and bounded back against the gunwale, lifting the ax as he rose. One swift blow, shortened and cramped by his position, was all he had time to deliver. Then his adversary was upon him with great, smothering paws that gripped his wrists and almost cracked the bones. The ax dropped from his hand, but he continued to struggle, kicking, twisting, fighting for time. And when he looked up he saw the moon flash on the white, grinning teeth of Congo, the deaf-mute.

There was a roar and a crash in the fore part of the boat. Abe was in the fight. He had laid hold of a four-foot oak log and was swinging it at the end of his long, powerful arms like a cudgel. "Allen, bring the guns!" he yelled, and leaped forward, tiger-like, upon the attackers.

Two of them went down under his rain of blows.

Three others closed on him savagely, striking with fists and knives, and for a second Tad could see only a struggling tangle of bodies on the landing. Then Abe rolled free and bounded to his feet once more. He was still swinging the great club, and he put all his sinewy young strength into every smashing blow. His wrath was terrible to see. Never in his life had he fought as he was fighting now. The black marauders broke and fled, stumbling, before that onslaught, and Abe followed, giving them no quarter.

All these events had taken place in the space of a few seconds. Still gripping Tad by the wrists, Congo had watched the swift, decisive battle between his confederates and the tall white boy. As they gave ground, he bared his teeth in a hideous snarl of fury. But he had his own work to do. The instant the landing was clear, the giant African seized Tad about the middle, swung him up under one huge arm, and sprang for the shoreward side of the boat. Locked in a death struggle with still another negro, Allen could give him no assistance. The boy caught at the gunwale as they went up, and clinging desperately with hands and feet, held his captor back for a second or two. Then his grip was wrenched loose, and the big black scaled the landing and started with him across the levee.

They were almost in the edge of the cane when Tad heard a thud of feet behind them. With a hoarse indrawing of breath, Congo turned at bay. Still clutching his prisoner with his left hand, the deaf-mute raised his tremendous right arm to demolish the pursuer.

It must have been a long time before he used that arm again. Abe, coming in on the run, struck downward swiftly, savagely, with the great oak cudgel. Under that crushing impact the bones parted with a dull crack, and Congo staggered, dropped Tad, and scuttled into the cane, the broken arm dangling horribly at his side.

The breath had been squeezed half out of the boy, but as he rose he managed to gasp ''Allen!'' and pushed Abe in the direction of the boat.

Allen, it seemed, had taken care of himself. He had been getting the better of the encounter when his antagonist had seen the others in flight and had jumped overboard and swum for it.

One half-naked black still lay on the levee, moaning piteously. He had fallen a victim to Abe's first attack, and there was an ugly bruise on his head. The fire went out of the big backwoodsman's eye as he came to the side of the wounded negro. Stooping, he carried him to the landing, washed his broken crown, and wrapped about his head a bandage made of a piece of his own torn shirt.

Gradually the man returned to full consciousness, and his groaning was quieted.

"We-all b'longs on de plantation above yere," he said, in response to Abe's questioning. "A white man done promise he gwine git us free if we he'p dat Congo nigger ketch de young white boy."

Abe looked at him grimly. "Kin you walk?" he said. The darky got painfully to his feet and stood looking at the tall young Hoosier in a palsy of terror.

"What we'd ought to do is tie ye up an' take ye on down to N'Orleans to jail," said Abe. "But in this fersaken country I s'pose they'd skin ye alive, down thar, an' that don't seem hardly fair, either. Go on—march yerself back whar ye belong, an' git thar quick, 'fore they find out ye're gone."

For a moment the negro stared at him, goggle-eyed with wonder. Then he was off, running up the levee as fast as his shaky legs could take him.

"Wal," said Allen, feeling of a barked elbow, "I reckon none of us is very sleepy right now." He went to the fire and threw on dry wood, poking it till a bright blaze sprang up. "Great wallopin' catamounts, Abe, but you sartin did give 'em what-for!" he chuckled. "Next time you aim to start a ruckus like that, I want to be sure I'm on your side.''

The big youngster ambled into the circle of firelight. ''You know me better'n that, Allen,'' he grinned. ''You never saw me *start* a fight in my life. But I figger when you do have to defend yerself, it pays to go after the other feller hard enough to put the fear o' the Lord in him.''

He turned to the boy by his side. ''How about ye, Tad—all right?''

''Fine,'' said Tad, ''but say—how about yourself?'' He seized his big friend by the arm and swung him half around in the firelight. ''Didn't you know you were bleeding?''

Abe put up a hand to his face and brought it away red and dripping. A deep gash over his right eye was bathing the side of his head and neck with blood.

''Huh!'' he laughed, ''I didn't even know I had that one. I've been thinkin' all this time it was sweat I was tastin'. Must ha' got cut with a knife in that fracas with the three of 'em, here on the landin'.''

He went down to the river and dipped his head in the water, after which Tad applied a tight bandage, and the bleeding soon stopped.

''Wal,'' said Allen, ''I don't reckon they'll be

back, but I ain't sleepy enough to turn in jest yet. What say we mosey along a few miles?''

"Suits me," Abe replied, "only before we go thar's one thing I want to look at.''

He selected a fat pine knot from the fire, and holding it as a torch to light his steps, walked slowly back to the edge of the cane, where Congo had vanished. They saw him stoop as if searching for something. Then he called to them. Looking where he pointed in the soft black earth, they saw a track—deep, gigantic, splay-toed—the same foot-print that had puzzled them that morning.

"That's the feller," said Abe. "You've seen him before, I reckon, Tad. Wasn't that Murrell's nig-ger?''

"Yes," said Tad, "he must have followed us all the way down from Natchez.''

"But how in time did he keep up with us?" asked Abe. "He couldn't ha' been aboard of a boat, could he?''

Tad told them of the canoe he had glimpsed, stealing between the islands when Abe was making his oar.

The big flatboatman nodded. "That was him, right enough," he said. "Only next time, Tad, don't be scairt to come right out with what you think. We might have saved ourselves a heap of exercise tonight if we'd known they was layin' for us.''

''Wonder if he planned to paddle clear back to Natchez with Tad in the dugout,'' said Allen as they went back across the levee

''No,'' Abe answered, thoughtfully. ''I b'lieve it was three of Murrell's gang that I saw gallopin' down the bluff road that afternoon. Most likely they're waitin' somewhere close, maybe in Baton Rouge, fer this tongueless, earless devil to bring Tad in. Let's drift along.''

They put out their fire, went aboard the broadhorn, and cast off the mooring-lines, glad to see the last of Madame Duquesne's plantation.

CHAPTER XVIII

Five or six miles below, they sighted a tiny, tree-clad island in midstream, and there once more made the boat fast. This time nothing interrupted their slumbers. They were under the west bank of the island, sheltered by overhanging branches, and the sun was high in the sky before they woke. It was the merry singing of a crew of river-men, floating past on their broad raft of steamboat fuel, that roused Tad. He sat up, saw that the morning was already well along, and gave Allen a dig in the ribs.

"Ahoy, you lubbers!" he cried. "Roll out! It's nearly noon."

He built the breakfast fire, washed himself, and went over to give Poke his morning greeting. As he started to maul the cub playfully, he saw him wince. The little bear limped and held up one forepaw in apparent pain. Looking closer, Tad found that it was bruised, as if it had been trodden on.

"Look at this, boys," he called. "Here's the real hero of the fight." And he told how Poke's growling had first awakened him in the night.

"A mighty good little b'ar," said Abe approvingly. "If that big-footed Congo stepped on him, though, he's lucky he didn't have his whole leg squashed."

Allen produced some bacon fat which was rubbed on the wound and which Poke at once set about licking off. After that he seemed to feel much better, and soon was his own droll self again.

Breakfast over, Abe bent his back to the oars, and they soon overhauled the wood-raft which had passed them. As the flatboat came alongside, one of the raft-men strolled over to the edge of the logs and hailed them. He was a tall, rangy Tennesseean in homespun.

"Big doin's in Baton Rouge las' night," said he, shooting a dark stream of tobacco juice into the yellow current.

"So?" replied Abe. "We tied up down river here a ways, an' slept peaceful."

"Hum, ye don't look it," said the raft-man, casting an eye at the red-tinged bandage around Abe's head. "I figgered maybe you-all was in the fight."

"What fight?" asked Allen.

"Ain't ye heard? Why, it seems there was a bunch o' river-men in Sancho's bar, down by the levee, an' Jack Murrell an' two of his gang come

in an' ordered drinks. Pretty soon somebody spot-
ted 'em, an' a row started. Murrell an' his men
shot their way out, an' they'd ha' got clean away,
only their hosses took fright and begun rarin'
around. 'Fore Bull Whaley could git mounted
somebody put a knife in him—killed him dead. An'
they grabbed Sam Jukes, too, an' put him in the
lock-up. Murrell had his luck with him, same as
usual. He gits on that ol' three-stockin' hoss o' his
an' goes a-sailin' off up the north road, belly to
the ground. He ain't got as many friends in Baton
Rouge as he has up river.''

''He's got plenty in Natchez,'' Abe replied. ''If
he don't break his neck on the way, he'll be safe
enough up thar.''

''Huh!'' laughed the raft hand. ''Break his
neck? Not him! He was born to be hung.''

They discussed the weather, the state of the
river, and General Jackson's chances in the coming presidential election. Allen traded a peck of
potatoes for some pipe tobacco, and they were
about to pass on, when the raft-man introduced a
new topic.

''Did ye see them notices stuck up around
Natchez an' Baton Rouge?'' he asked. ''Five thousand dollars reward fer findin' some boy that's

lost. A lad 'bout the size an' looks o' the one you got thar, I should say.'' He cast a keen glance in Tad's direction.

Tad grinned and stood up, stretching, so that his ragged clothes and sunburnt legs and arms became visible.

"Yeah?" he remarked. "Some rich city kid from back east, wasn't he?"

If the Tennessee man had had any suspicions, they were allayed. He nodded. "Some feller was tellin' how a broadhorn steerer from up the Ohio had done got hold o' the boy an' was boun' to git the reward," said he.

"Humph," grunted Abe, noncommittally, and dug deep with the oars. The *Katy Roby* went lumbering downstream, leaving the raft astern.

"So long," called Allen and Tad. "See you in New Orleans."

"Gosh," chuckled Allen as they drew out of earshot. "You sure fooled him that time, son. In that rig I doubt if yer own Pappy'd know ye."

Notwithstanding the late start, Abe had put twenty miles behind them by the time Allen announced that the noon meal was ready.

He stretched his big arms wearily and wiped away the sweat that was streaming out from beneath his piratical-looking bandage.

"Wal," he said, as he sat down, "I promised Tad I'd git him to New Orleans 'most as soon as the mail, an' you noticed no steamboats have passed us yet."

"Don't worry," said Allen. "They will. I jest heard one whistlin' up above the bend, four or five minutes ago."

Sure enough, before Abe had swallowed the last of his tea, they heard a loud blast close astern, and one of the stately white river steamers came plowing down the channel. Allen jumped to the sweep and Abe to the bow oars, and they had barely time to swing the *Katy Roby* over toward the right, when the nose of the big craft went sweeping by.

Abe held the flatboat on her course as the wash from the paddles rocked her. Then he turned, leaning on his oars, and watched the steamer bear away to the east, rounding a bend.

"Maybe she won't beat us by so much, at that," said the big rower with a laugh. "I've got a sort of an idee that that narrow cut, ahead thar, will save us a few miles."

Instead of following the steamboat around the curve of the main river, Abe steered straight for the mouth of the cut, where a channel a hundred feet wide led between low banks of willow. The current flowing through this cut was not as rapid as they had found it in some of the chutes farther north, and Tad remarked on the fact.

"I suppose it's just because the whole river moves slower down here near the Gulf," he said.

Abe made no reply but pulled steadily forward between the close banks rank with tropical vegetation. For a mile or more the cut ran fairly straight. Then it began to twist disconcertingly, first west, then north, then west and south again.

Big live oaks and dark, mysterious-looking cypresses began to appear along the shores. The water, instead of having the yellow hue they had seen for the last thousand miles, was a dark brown, but clear enough to see the snags and weed-clumps two or three feet below the surface.

Rounding still another bend, they came suddenly on a wide reach, unlike any section of the river they had yet encountered.

Enormous trees shut it in on both sides with high, thick walls of green. There were flowering vines twining high into the branches of these trees, and in some places the vermilion-tinted blossoms glowed like a flame against the dark background.

Along the shores, in the edge of the stream, grew other flowers—solid masses of pink and

purple water hyacinths, like low islands of bloom.
A little breeze came up the reach from the south,
and Tad saw a section of one of these islands de-
tach itself and go drifting up the channel like a
gay-colored pleasure barge.

A blue heron almost as tall as a man looked up
from his frog-hunting and rose on great silent
wings, flapping away to the depths of the cypress
swamp. There were no songs of birds to break
the funereal stillness. Even the water was still. If
it had any movement, it was so sluggish that the
eye could hardly detect it.

Abe had stopped rowing and stood on the fore
deck looking about him. The quietness affected all
of them strangely. They felt like speaking in
whispers.

"Gosh," murmured Allen, "ain't it purty here!
Spooky, though."

"It's purty, right enough," Abe answered.
"But it's not the Mississippi. We've got into a
slack-water, somehow."

"That's a fact," said Allen. "It don't seem
quite like the river, does it? Jiminy Pete! Look
a' thar! They's more alligators in this place than
catfish in our creek back home."

The roaring challenge of a bull 'gator came
from down the reach, and others answered all

along the bank. Shattering the quiet of the place and reëchoing from the tall cypresses, the sound was almost terrifying in its intensity. Hardly had it died away when the boys heard the report of a gun, close at hand, and a puff of blue smoke drifted out from behind a little point.

Allen would have rushed under the shelter to get his own fowling-piece, but Abe held up a warning hand.

"Wait," he said in a low voice. "That wasn't meant fer us. Here he comes, now."

Past the point there shot a long, low dugout canoe. A man knelt a little aft of the middle, driving her along with short, quick paddle strokes. As he caught sight of the broadhorn he paused with paddle lifted, as if in astonishment. Then he changed his course and came slowly toward them.

They saw as he approached that he was a handsome young fellow, with olive skin and long dark hair—a typical Creole of the river parishes. In the canoe just in front of him lay a fine silver-mounted shotgun, and beside it they saw the snowy white plumage of an egret.

"Howdy, friend," said Abe. "Could you tell us about whar we might be, now?"

The youth looked them over calmly and a trifle patronizingly.

"I thing you come from up the big riv'," said he. "*Mais,* you done los' the way, huh? You mus' come t'rough the cut. Dat ain' righd. The Mississip', she make a beeg ben'. This w'ere you are, it is Bayou Tante Lisette."

"Thank ye," said Abe. "I reckon that means we've jest got to pull back." He dipped deeply with the starboard oar and swung the blunt nose of the flatboat around.

"Adieu," said the Creole with a grave little bow, and turned his canoe down the bayou, in the opposite direction.

Around the tortuous bends Abe retraced his course. It was hard rowing, and he had very little sympathy from the rest of the crew.

"Seems to me," snickered Allen, "I recall a feller up near the Wabash mouth that got a smart answer when he asked whar'bouts he was. Pore devil of a mover, he was, too, with a hull family o' kids—not a tip-top, high-rollin' river hand like you."

Abe grinned good-naturedly. "That was up in God's own country, whar I knew a thing or two," he answered. "We all make mistakes when we git in a strange place. But you kin gamble on it, I won't make this one twice."

The afternoon was half gone when they got back

into the main river. Tad had translated the French name of the picturesque backwater into which they had blundered, and Allen made frequent remarks about Abe's excursion to "Aunt Lizzie's Bay," as he called it. The long-legged Hoosier stood it for a while in silence, then made a casual reference to Memphis and Natchez that effectually silenced his tormentor. Abe had been rowing almost without a stop since morning and as soon as they reached the broad yellow flood of the Mississippi once more, he turned the oars over to Allen.

"I'm glad, as a matter o' fact, that we got in thar," the big backwoodsman told Tad, as he sat down to rest. "Fer years I've heard tell, from the men on the river, about these bayous that go stragglin' off from the big channel an' wander through the swamps into the Gulf. Now I've seen one, which I most likely never would, if we hadn't lost our way."

After supper Abe mounted the fore deck again, and they pushed on steadily until dusk fell. There was a small landing with two or three houses in sight on the west bank, and to it they directed their course. Other flatboats were moored along the levee. As Abe tied up close to them, he hailed the occupants of the nearest craft.

"How fur do ye figger it is to New Orleans?"
he asked.

"Not more'n twenty-five mile," the other flatboat hand replied. "We aim to make it by noon."

They spread their blankets and said their good-
nights. Tad could not go to sleep at first for thinking of the morrow. Only a half-day's journey to
New Orleans and his father! For the twentieth
time his eager mind anticipated their meeting.
Would he be recognized? Allen had said even his
own Pappy wouldn't know him, but he had no fear
of that. Tad could guess at Allen's thoughts as he
lay there on the verge of sleep. They would be full
of the Creole girls and the pretty quadroons, and
what a dashing figure he would cut amongst them
in his store clothes.

And Abe—what was he thinking, rolled in his
blanket on the forward deck, under the stars? Not
about girls. Tad knew him well enough to be sure
of that. The big young river-man had ideas, queer,
searching ideas about people—all sorts of people,
rich and poor—about niggers, even—and about
right and wrong. He wrestled with them just as he
had wrestled with the Tennessee bear-hunter, long
and hard, until they were down.

Tad had some inkling of what this trip meant to

him—getting out of the little backwoods world where he had been raised, and seeing the great valley and the cities of the South. He thought a lot of Abe. He liked the big, homely, raw-boned youngster better than any friend he had ever had. He hoped his father would like him, too. Perhaps he could give him a good job in the New Orleans office. Perhaps . . . but sleep overtook Tad in the middle of his perhapsing, and he was kidnapped over the border into dreamland.

CHAPTER XIX

Tad was roused, as he had been on that eventful morning in the Ohio, nearly four weeks earlier, by Allen's voice raised in song:

> "Hard upon the beach oar—
> She moves too slow!
> All the way to New Orleans,
> Lo-o-ong time ago-o!"

It was barely daylight; yet the breakfast fire was snapping merrily, and Abe was busy preparing for a start. As the boy washed himself, he saw signs of similar activity on board the other broadhorns, and by the time they were finishing the morning meal, one or two of the craft had already taken their departure.

Abe sent a loud challenge after them as he cast loose the mooring-line, and in another thirty seconds he was boiling along in their wake. It was a brisk morning, with a little breeze from down river ruffling the water. Everybody's spirits were high, and for the next half hour all the rowers put the best they had into the race. By the end of that time Abe's brawny strokes had carried the *Katy Roby* so far into the lead that there was no longer

any hope of catching her, and the other boats settled down to their normal gait.

Not so Abe. He kept a wrinkle of foam under the
flatboat's square bow for two hours without a let-
up. When at last he snatched a moment's rest, he
explained his haste to Tad.

"You've eaten your last meal o' hog meat an'
johnny-cake fer a spell, son," said he. "I aim to
git you down thar in time fer you to have a civilized dinner with your Paw."

In spite of the boy's remonstrances, his big
friend kept up the pace. And sure enough, by a
little after ten o'clock they came in sight of the
upper outposts of the city.

Along the left bank the vegetable gardens gave
way to scattered hovels, and they in turn to houses
—streets of them—closely built, all sheltered behind the broad rampart of the levee. Then came
the steamboat landings, and all three of the *Katy
Roby's* crew stared in open-mouthed wonder at
the ranks of tall stacks and the glistening white
and brasswork of more than thirty steamers
moored there, noses in to the bank.

Even along the water fronts of New York and
Philadelphia, Tad had never seen such swarming
activity as he witnessed here. Hundreds of blacks
toiled in the sun, rolling molasses barrels and cot-

ton bales. Directing them were sharp-faced Yankee merchants and brawny steamboat mates, with an occasional soft-spoken Creole or gesticulating Spaniard.

Anchored in the curving channel of the river were sailing-ships, big and little, flying the flags of all the world. There were heavy British merchantmen, Dutch and Danish brigs, fast-sailing, tall-masted ships from Boston and New York and Baltimore, French barques, trim West Indian schooners, and slovenly little lateen-rigged boats from the bays and inlets along the Gulf.

And then Tad saw the flatboat fleet. For the better part of a mile they lay along the levee, four, six —sometimes ten deep—a solid mass of keel-boats, broadhorns, and scows. It was impossible to count them, but there must have been not less than four or five hundred in sight. And the noise that rose from them was terrific, as newcomers hailed each other and fought for places.

"Whew!" said Abe in some dismay. "Thicker'n ants at a camp-meetin' picnic, ain't they? How in time are we goin' to git nigh this town?"

At that moment, almost opposite the *Katy Roby's* bow, a keel-boat was working its way out of the tangle of craft, and Abe backed water and stood by, ready to enter the space she was about to leave. By skillful jockeying he worked the nose of the flatboat into the hole and succeeded in getting in until only one broadhorn separated them from the shore.

The stout Kentuckian who owned her looked the newcomers over without any signs of welcome.

"Hyah you-all come a-crowdin' in," he grumbled, "an' next I s'pose you'll want to fasten yo' worm-eaten tub on to mine. Is that so?"

"I'm askin' you," grinned Abe. "Will you do us that favor?"

The Kentucky man eyed the big Hoosier from his worn moccasins to his rugged, fighting face still topped by the blood-stained bandage.

"I reckon so," said he, and grinned in his turn. "Whar 'bouts you from?"

While Abe was telling him he passed the *Katy Roby's* line across the deck of the other boat and took a hitch around one of the mooring-posts on shore.

"I was born in your state, myself," Abe told the Kentuckian. "My Paw moved us across the river when I was seven."

"Too bad—too bad!" commiserated the stocky flatboatman. "Still, it's somethin' to have come from Kentucky, even if you had the misfortune not to stay thar."

He offered Abe a drink from his jug of red-eye, and when it was politely declined he seemed surprised, but not offended. From that time on he regarded the Hoosier crew as friends and allies.

"Now then, Tad," said Abe when all was snug, "we'll go straight ashore an' see if we kin locate your Pappy's office. Allen'll take keer of the cargo fer a spell, won't ye, Allen?"

The young man in question appeared sheepishly from under the tarpaulin, with his razor and brush in his hand. "Sure," he answered. "I jes' thought I'd shave me up a little, first off, so when I go ashore I kin talk to the commission merchants 'thout lookin' too much like a backwoods jay."

Abe and Tad scrambled across the Kentucky broadhorn and stepped out on the wide, sun-baked levee top. Behind them the water, high with the April freshets, was a good ten feet above the level of the streets to which they now descended. It gave Tad a queer feeling of insecurity to see the twin stacks of the steamers standing high above the church steeples. But that was only a momentary fancy. His attention was centered on his present errand, and he whistled merrily as he hurried along beside Abe.

The towering young Hoosier's strides ate up distance surprisingly, and they were soon well into the business section of the city. Tad asked a Creole shopkeeper, in good French, where they might find the Rue St. Louis, and was told, in funny but understandable English, that it was the next street but one. Going forward as directed, they quickly found not only the street but the number they wanted. It was a large, severe-looking building of three stories, with none of the pretty tracery of iron balconies that adorned so many of the houses.

The two lads entered the public hallway and climbed the stairs to the second floor. Tad felt a joyous pounding under his ribs at the sight of the name JEREMIAH HOPKINS lettered on the door. He opened it with trembling fingers and entered, Abe following at his heels.

To his disappointment, his father was nowhere in sight. At the rear of the room a big desk and chair stood—vacant. Two or three clerks sat on tall stools, scribbling away at their ledgers. A dapper young secretary with a small mustache and a supercilious air came forward to the rail.

"I'm Thaddeus Hopkins," said Tad. "Isn't my father here?"

The man seemed not at all impressed. He stroked his chin with one hand and smiled cynically.

"So you're the boy himself, eh?" said he. "Let's see, you're the third—no, the fourth—that's been here, and you aren't the likeliest-looking one of the lot, at that. You've come for the reward, I suppose?"

"No," Tad replied, somewhat nettled by the fellow's attitude. "I haven't come for any reward. I've come to see my father. Where is he?"

The secretary scowled. "Now see here," said he, "don't give me any more of your impudence, or I'll have you arrested. Mr. Hopkins went up river some days ago—to follow up an important clue," he added weightily, as if to settle the matter.

Abe looked at Tad and grinned, and seeing him, the young man with the mustache flew into a rage. "Get out of here!" he cried. "Get out at once, before I call the police. And if I catch you in here again I'll use a cane on you!"

Tad's sense of humor got the better of his wrath, at that. He stopped short of the hot answer he had started to make, and laughed, with Abe, at the sheer ridiculousness of the affair. They went slowly to the door. On the threshold Tad turned and looked once more at the secretary, who was now fairly purple with indignation.

"All right," said the boy, trying to hold back

his laughter, "you'd better keep that cane handy, because we'll be back." And he closed the door quietly in the face of the sputtering clerk.

When they reached the street once more, Abe looked at Tad with a droll expression and shook his head.

"I can't rightly blame the feller," he chuckled. "I never thought how we were goin' to look, an' you wouldn't be taken fer any swell Easterner, ye know."

Tad glanced down at his costume. It was the first time he had even thought about his appearance for weeks. And as he realized how he must have looked to the dapperly attired young underling in his father's office, he burst into another shout of merriment.

His shirt was in rags, with one sleeve torn out entirely at the shoulder. The butternut breeches of Abe's purchase had stood up better under hard service, but even they were tattered in several places, and very dirty. His bare feet and legs still showed the marks of the many scrapes and scratches he had got in his adventure with the outlaws. And he knew that his skin, tanned to the color of an Indian's, and his uncombed thatch of hair, must give him anything but a prepossessing appearance.

"I reckon what ye really need," said Abe, "is a bran' new suit o' store clothes, an' a hair-cut. Then maybe some stockin's an' shoes an' a necktie might help. 'Bout twelve dollars an' a half in gov'-ment notes, an' you'd be the real Tad Hopkins ag'in, 'stead o' jest a plain, ornery little river-rat. The only question now is, whar are we a-goin' to git that much cash? Speakin' fer myself, jest at the present moment I haven't got even one lonesome cent. Looks like I'd have to break my promise an' take ye back to eat aboard the boat ag'in."

They wandered through the hot streets, picturesque but smelly, and came at length to the levee market, where long rows of booths under brightly striped canopies displayed eatables of every sort. There were rice and green corn, ginger, all kinds of berries, oranges and bananas, live fowls tied in threes and hanging by their legs, quail and other game, fish and shrimps from the Gulf; and crawfish, sold by wrinkled old Choctaw Indian women.

At some of the stalls mulattoes held up chocolate in big steaming cups, and from others came the delicious odor of hot rice and gumbo.

"Hm," said Abe, "'twon't do to hang 'round here very long. I'm commencin' to git mighty hungry."

They threaded their way through the crowds of

Creole housewives with their black servants carrying market baskets, and emerged in front of a long warehouse opening on the levee near the steamboat landing.

Before this warehouse stood a two-horse dray, partly loaded with barrels and boxes, and around it were three negroes apparently waiting for something. A well-dressed, elderly white man fumed up and down meanwhile, and expressed his opinion of the colored race in no uncertain terms. As Tad and Abe drew near, he addressed his remarks to them.

"Look at this," he snorted. "For fifteen minutes these good-for-nothing niggers of mine have been standing around waiting for some one to fetch a plank so that they can roll a barrel of indigo on to this wagon. The *Maid of Camberwell* sails on the next tide, and we have to haul the goods a mile to where her lighter is moored. If these blankety-blank sons of Ham were worth their salt, they could hoist the barrel up by hand, and I'd have some chance of making this ship. The next cargo for Liverpool may not go out for a month."

Abe strolled up to the huge blue-stained barrel and tipped it a little with his hand.

''How much is it worth to you to git it loaded?''
he asked the owner.

''How much! I'd give a dollar to have that indigo on the dray,'' he replied.

''All right,'' said Abe, ''that's a bargain.''

He rolled the barrel up to the rear of the wagon, spat on his hands, placed his feet carefully and put his arms, back, and knees into a single mighty heave. With a resounding thump, five hundred pounds of indigo landed on the tailboard and were rolled forward to stand beside the rest of the load.

Abe dusted off his hands and jumped lightly to the ground. He was not even breathing hard.

The merchant was still standing in the same spot, open-mouthed with astonishment.

''Great heavens, man!'' he stammered, when he could find words. ''Why, it's amazing, sir—astounding! I can't believe my eyes! Here—'' and he thrust a hand into his pocket—''I'll be better than my word. Here's a two-dollar note.''

Abe hesitated. ''I 'greed to do it fer one,'' he said. ''Still, if you mean it, I'll accept your offer. The boy, here, an' I—we kin sure use it.'' He took the bill, thanked the merchant, and they went on.

''Tad,'' grinned the long-shanked Hoosier, as he gave the boy's arm a squeeze, ''by the sun an' by my in'ard feelin's it 'pears to be past noon. I vote we head straight fer one o' those rice an' gumbo places.''

They retraced their steps and were soon served with bowls of the savory stuff, ladled out of a huge copper pot by a motherly-looking quadroon woman.

Tad smacked his lips. ''Mm, tastes good, doesn't it?'' he said. ''How much did it cost?''

''Four cents apiece,'' Abe answered. ''We could live ashore quite a spell on our two dollars, couldn't we? Golly! Two dollars! That's the easiest money I ever made. Why, think—it's the same as a whole week's pay navigatin' the *Katy Roby!*''

They bought half a dozen oranges as a special treat—Abe had never eaten one in his life—and went back to the place where their flatboat was tied up.

Allen looked up in surprise from the pans he was washing. ''You back, Tad?'' he exclaimed. ''I figgered nex' time I saw you, it would be in one o' them shiny two-hoss carriages with a brass-buttoned nigger up in front.''

They related the happenings of the morning, and Allen roared with laughter. ''Wal,'' said he, ''we're bound to stay here fer a couple more days anyhow. None of the commission men kin handle

the cargo short o' that time. An' you're welcome
to sleep on board here as long as you've a mind
to.''

''Thanks,'' said Tad, ''I guess I'll have to do
that, until Dad comes back from up river.''

While he was ashore Allen had left the boat under the guardianship of their neighbor, the Kentucky man. ''I don't see him anywheres around
now,'' said he, ''but you folks don't need to stay
here. I'll watch the stuff this afternoon, an' then
you kin take charge after supper. Reckon I'd
rather go ashore in the evenin', when it's cooler,
anyway.''

Abe and Tad laughed at him, but they were glad
to fall in with his idea, for both of them wanted to
see the town. They made such repairs as they could
to their clothes, and Abe hauled out from some
hiding-place a treasured old coonskin cap.

''This'll keep the sun off my head,'' he explained, ''an' I reckon in the city it looks better'n
no hat at all.''

Tad tried to reason with him, but it was to no
purpose. Abe topped off his six feet four of homespun shirt, buckskin breeches, and moccasins with
the moth-eaten fur cap, and they set forth.

CHAPTER XX

New Orleans, in that spring of 1828, was as strange and fascinating a place as ever two boys wandered through on a sunny afternoon.

It was a big town—big even to the eyes of Tad, who had seen other cities. Fifty thousand people lived in it, and there were usually two or three thousand sailors from the ships in port besides perhaps five thousand wild, roistering river-men jostling through the streets.

With half the commerce of the vast Mississippi Valley pouring through it, New Orleans was growing and spreading like one of its own rank tropical weeds. It had swept past the walls and moats of the old French-Spanish city years before, and now its newer sections filled most of the crescent-shaped bend above the original town.

It was along the levee of this new part of the city that the flatboat fleet was moored, and the first mile that Abe and Tad traversed was through raw, fresh-built streets that had little of the picturesque about them. Only here and there ancient French houses, set among great trees, showed where the country estates of rich Creoles had once stood.

But when they crossed Canal Street they found themselves breathing a different atmosphere. There was none of the bustling newness of the American quarter. The houses, large and small, had cozy walled gardens and shady balconies, and even the flagstones seemed to drowse in the warm sunshine.

From this residential district they bore southward again and came to a region of old shops, old offices, and here and there a venerable church or public building.

There seemed to be few people stirring at this time of day in the more ancient part of the city. But as they neared the water front they found the streets busier.

At one place in particular a crowd seemed to be collected. It was a ramshackle old hotel building with a driveway leading to an inner courtyard. On the sidewalk before the building and passing in and out were little knots and groups of men, talking and smoking Havana cigars. By far the larger number of these men were prosperous-looking planters from up and down the river and the outlying parishes. They were easily distinguishable by their broad-brimmed felt hats and riding-boots, and by their talk, which was of crops and horses and negroes—mostly of negroes.

Two or three printed posters were tacked up on the wall of the building, and Tad strolled over to read them. One said:

"Runaway—a bright mulatto boy named Cassius, about eighteen years old, strong and large. Will probably head north, as he was Kentucky raised."

Another advertised: "For sale, a mighty valuable woman, twenty-five with three likely children. A bargain for the lot."

The third and largest poster was what particularly attracted Tad's attention, however. As he finished reading it he beckoned to Abe. It said:

"On these premises, every Tuesday and Saturday afternoon, will be held regular auctions of negroes. We have now on hand a large, well selected stock of field hands, house boys, cooks, seamstresses, etc., and will sell as low as any house in New Orleans. Fresh arrivals keep our stock in prime condition at all times, and we have our own jail and yard for boarding them."

"Abe," Tad asked, "isn't this Saturday?"

"Let's see, so 'tis," responded Abe. "Want to go in?"

Tad hesitated. ''Not much,'' said he, ''and yet it's one of the things to see in New Orleans.''

Abe led the way through the driveway into the courtyard. The throng of planters and city men inside made way grudgingly for the tall young backwoodsman in his outlandish costume, and Abe edged forward until he reached a place where both Tad and himself had a view of the auction platform.

The auctioneer was a big, red-faced, jolly-looking man who spoke in a loud voice and was given to coarse jokes when he found the bidding too slow to suit him.

On the ground beside the block stood a row of eight or ten negroes awaiting their turn to be sold. Occasionally one of the planters would go up to a slave, poke him in the ribs, feel of his arms and legs and look him over much as a buyer of cattle would do. In the group of negroes Tad saw a bent old woman with gray hair, one or two handsome young mulatto girls, a smart-looking saddle-colored boy with the manners of a Virginia-bred house servant, and half a dozen coal-black Guinea negroes, scantily clothed in dingy cotton. On the faces of these last there was a wild, stupid, frightened look, quite different from the lazy good humor that Tad had always associated with their race. When he looked closely he saw that one staggered a little as if from weakness, and on the ankles of three or four he could make out raw, new scars—chain and fetter scars.

Abe had seen them, too. "They're just off the slaver," he whispered. "Smuggled in through the bayous—bet they haven't been ashore more'n a week. Look at that pore devil that's sick!"

The auctioneer had one of the young mulattto women on the block now. He pinched her sportively, chucked her under the chin, and made some ribald remark heard only by the men just below him. Then he brought down his gavel with a thump.

"Well, gents, what am I offered?" he inquired genially. "A thousand dollars as a starter wouldn't be a bit too much for this wench. They don't come no better built. A mite broad in the shoulders perhaps, but that's what a good house-work nigger needs. Look her over, now. Take yo' time. Now, who'll offer a thousand? No? Not yet, eh? Well, start her at five hundred, then. What d'ye say? Will the tall gentleman in the fur cap make it five hundred for this prime yaller gal?"

There was a titter in the crowd, but Abe remained silent and impassive while the bidding went forward. Only Tad, looking up at him sidewise, could see a hard white ridge under the tanned skin of his jaw.

The girl was sold at last, and the auctioneer replaced her with the feeble old grandmother, who was poked and prodded into straightening her bent back a trifle and stepping briskly about on the block.

"Now here's one that's a bargain," began the loud, droning voice of the seller. "There's three or four years of good hard work under her black hide yet. Now I'll take a starting offer of forty dollars. Who'll say forty?"

Abe nudged the boy at his side. "Come on," he muttered. "I can't stand any more of this."

Once outside, the tall young river-man took off his cap and wiped the sweat from his forehead with his sleeve.

"Tad," he said, almost fiercely, "it's all wrong—this whole slavery business—as wrong as murder. Let's get away from that place."

He was sober and silent as they crossed Jackson Square, the old Place d'Armes of the Creoles, and it was not until they had walked up the levee for some distance and were nearing the flatboat moorings again that his old good humor returned.

"Golly," he marveled. "Aren't they a sight?

I bet ye could walk a mile on nothin' but boats an' never wet a toe.''

They found Allen ready to set forth on his evening's adventure. He was attired in all his finery and had his hair slicked down so that it shone.

''What the Sam Hill is that on yer head?'' asked Abe. ''Lard?''

''No,'' answered Allen proudly, ''that's genuwine b'ar's grease. I borrowed it from a Tennessee man—third boat up.''

''Say, speakin' o' b'ars,'' said Abe, ''whar's that good-fer-nothin' Poke?''

''Oh,'' Allen replied, a trifle shamefacedly, ''he done pulled his staple an' walked off 'fore I could ketch him. He was clear up on the levee an' headin' west, last sight I had of him.''

Abe looked at him with withering scorn. ''You must ha' taken a lot o' care o' the boat,'' said he. ''It's a durn wonder the pork an' provisions didn't climb out o' the hold an' walk off, too.''

These and other sarcastic remarks made Allen's supper uncomfortable, and he was in a hurry to leave as soon as it was eaten.

Abe and Tad watched the young Hoosier dandy depart down the levee, then set to work straightening up the boat. They enjoyed the cool evening breeze for a while, and when the first stars appeared, they spread their blankets and went to sleep.

What time Allen returned they did not know, but he was there in the bed next morning, far too drowsy to do more than open one eye when they called him to breakfast.

They heard church bells tolling in different parts of the city and remembered that it was Sunday morning. That was the only indication of the day, for as the town awoke there was anything but a Sabbath calm in the air.

All the saloons, dance halls, and gambling-places along the water front were open for business, and the thousands of river-men and sailors thronging the levee brought them plenty of it. Above the din of shouting, fighting, and merry-making, Abe had to talk loud to make himself heard.

"Allen won't want to go ashore again fer a spell," he said. "We kin leave the boat to him an' go lookin' fer that cub o' yours."

Tad, who had been considerably cast down by the loss of his pet, was eager to follow Abe's suggestion. They took their way along the water front, asking people they met if they had seen the little black bear. For the most part the question was greeted with jeers or with blank astonishment. But once they encountered a half-drunken raft hand who testified somewhat hazily to having seen not merely one bear but a pair of them, dragging chains after them, and moving in the direction of the steamboat moorings. And a voluble Creole in a little tobacco shop told them that a bear "so beeg as a cow" had looked in the door at him, growled, and passed on.

"That b'ar knows what he's about," chuckled Abe. "He aims to travel back to Tennessee by steamboat—that's sartin."

A little farther on they asked their question of a British sailorman, and he nodded and pointed up the nearest street.

"Aye," said he, "that must be the one they caught this mornin' and are goin' to bait with dogs. There's a bit of excitement up at the public 'ouse yonder. Perhaps they've started already."

As the two lads hurried forward, they saw that the "bit of excitement" had more the look of a general street fight.

A crowd of fifteen or twenty ark hands, all riotously drunk, were milling about a smaller group that seemed to be made up chiefly of steamboat men. In the center was a short, sturdy Irishman, with his blue cap cocked at a pugnacious angle and the joy of battle in his blue eyes. Tad would have recognized that freckled face anywhere. It was

Dennis McCann, the mate of the *Ohio Belle*. And crouched between his bowed seaman's legs was little black Poke.

Already fists were flying, and matters looked bad for the steamboat men when Abe hit the fringe of the mob like a tornado, with Tad right at his heels. Some he knocked down with his fists, some he flung out of his path, and those who came back for more were treated to a double dose. The vicious flank attack confused the backwoodsmen, and before they could rally, the steamboat crew were pummeling them from in front. In a moment the battle had turned into a rout. Some ran down the street with the victors at their heels, and others took refuge in the saloon.

"Here," panted Abe to McCann, "let's take the b'ar an' git out o' this 'fore they git together ag'in."

To the little Irishman, who had been slugging away blindly in the middle of the mêlée, all wearers of buckskin and homespun were enemies.

"An' who the divil might you be?" he growled, bristling.

"Hold on," interposed Tad. "Don't you know me? You gave me breakfast on the *Ohio Belle* a month ago."

McCann's eyes bulged. "Sure an' it's the lad

that disappeared!" he cried. "It's himself that's in it, the saints be praised! Come to me, b'y, an' let me look at ye!"

He wrung Tad's hand with both of his, and then gripped Abe's big fist when the backwoods youth was introduced as a friend.

"So the little cub here is yours?" said McCann. "Begorra, he come a-strayin' past our moorin' last night, an' thinks I, we'll have a mascot aboard the *Ohio Belle*. So I catches him, an' ties him to a beam. But this mornin' he was gone again, an' when I come ashore I seen a bunch o' these roustabouts gettin' ready to murther him with dogs. So I steps in an' grabs him, an' that's that. But come on board the boat with me now, an' tell me how it comes ye're not restin' this minute at the bottom o' the Ohio."

They followed the mate to his cabin on the steamer, and Tad had his first chance to unfold the long tale of his adventures. As he described how he was held prisoner by the outlaws, McCann rose and paced the room.

"Begob," said he, "an' it's sorry I am that I didn't know the man Murrell was aboard. Think o' the grand chances I had to bash him with a belayin'-pin. An' him cleanin' out the gamblers with the money he robbed you of!"

Tad concluded his story by telling of the treatment he had received at his father's office.

"Mr. McCann," Abe put in, "I reckon you might be able to identify the lad. They seem powerful hard to satisfy, but they sure ought to take your word."

"Faith, an' I'll try," said the steamboat man. "I'll go with ye tomorrer mornin' whin the office opens. But I've got the afternoon off today. I'll take ye 'round the town."

And when they had been all over the *Ohio Belle* and Tad had shown Abe the stateroom where he had slept and the rail over which he had been thrown, they left Poke securely chained, and started forth with the little Irishman as their guide.

CHAPTER XXI

Dennis McCann knew a lot about New Orleans. He had been spending days exploring the town every time he got into port, and there were few corners into which he had not penetrated. He took Tad and Abe a good ten miles that Sunday afternoon, and Tad, at least, was footsore before they finished.

First the mate of the *Ohio Belle* led them northward and eastward through the hot streets to the green flats at the rear of the town. As they went they were joined by other groups bound in the same direction, and soon they found themselves part of a huge throng, all moving steadily out toward the Congo Plains.

Rising above the dust of the crowds, they saw the rough timber amphitheater of the bull ring, and near it the gaudy-hued canvas of a huge tent. There was no bullfight scheduled for that day, but Cayetano's famous circus was in full swing.

Pushing forward with the throng, they entered the big top, where snake-charmers and sleek-skinned yellow dancers vied for attention with two-headed calves, fat ladies, and real wild animals in cages.

The latter appealed most to Abe. He had read of lions in *Aesop's Fables,* but never had he beheld one nor heard one roar, and Tad laughed to see the six-foot Hoosier jump and shiver when that bass thunder sounded behind him.

When they had finished with the circus, McCann led the way to another marvel—the roadbed of the New Orleans and Pontchartrain Railway which was to connect the city with the lake on the north.

This was to be one of the first steam railroads in the world, and Abe and Tad looked with awe on the preparations for it. People even said that with a steam engine on wheels, such as the owners proposed to run, you could pull half a dozen big wagons at once along level rails!

"As strong as six teams of horses, Abe! Do you believe that?" asked Tad.

"Yes," said the backwoodsman, "reckon I do, after seein' a steamboat work. But when they tell me this thing is *faster* than horses, I'll admit I'm a leetle bit doubtful."

They came back in the cool of the early evening and strolled along the levee above the town to the park-like drive where a long parade of carriages wound among the China trees. Planters and their wives, aristocratic Creole families, and the beautiful women of the free quadroon caste went smiling by, behind their smartly trotting horses.

From a little lake a flock of pelicans rose on heavy wings and flapped away across the sunset to their nests. Fireflies began to twinkle in the gathering dusk. A guitar was strumming softly near by.

"Golly," murmured Tad, "I shouldn't wonder if Heaven must be something like this!"

Abe's face was overspread by a grin. "Only," said he, "in Heaven the folks have wings, an' the mosquitoes don't." And he emphasized his remark by slapping himself on the back of the neck.

They strolled back through a summer night that was breathlessly hot in the narrow streets and cooled by a little breeze along the levee.

"Huh," mused Abe. "Here it's actin' like mid-July, an' in a couple o' weeks I'll be back in May again, with the trees jes' comin' into full leaf an' the lilacs hardly done bloomin' in the dooryards."

"When'll ye be leavin'?" asked McCann. "We've got 'most a cargo now, an' if ye were ready by tomorrer, say, I might get ye a berth an' a chance to earn yer board loadin' wood fer the engines."

Abe thanked him. "First of all," said he, "I

want to see Tad out o' this scrape. An' second,
I've got to keep my partner, Allen Gentry, from
gittin' *into* one, when he sells his goods. After that
I'd be pleased to ship with you.''

As they parted from McCann at the gangplank
of the *Ohio Belle,* the little Irishman pointed to
Poke, snoring comfortably at the end of his chain
on deck.

''See,'' he laughed, ''the little spalpeen is right
at home. I'll give ye three dollars fer him.''

Tad considered a moment. He could hardly hope
to keep the cub with him, either in the city or at
school, while with McCann he knew the little bear
would be in good hands.

''Right,'' he answered regretfully, and the
transaction was completed, then and there. As the
boy trudged along at Abe's side, he pulled the
money out of his pocket.

''Here,'' said he, ''this'll pay for those pants,
Abe. And anyway, the bear was really yours. You
saved his life and then wrestled for him.''

''No sech of a thing!'' said Abe warmly. ''That
b'ar b'longed to you.''

But Tad was adamant, and his big friend finally
took the money, on condition that he should buy
them both a supper out of it. Accordingly they
stopped at the next tavern and ordered a meal.

The table at which they sat was at the rear of the sanded floor near one end of the bar. A cosmopolitan throng of sailors and up-river men were drinking and quarreling noisily along the mahogany rail, and Tad watched them while Abe picked the bones of his fricasseed chicken.

Suddenly, in the crowd, he caught sight of a familiar back and saw a hand filled with banknotes waving in the air.

"Quick, Abe!" said the boy. "Isn't that Allen with all that money?"

The long-shanked backwoodsman turned, pushing back his chair, and looked where Tad was pointing. At that moment a big German sailor reached over the heads of the eager fellows who surrounded Allen, seized his wrist with one hand, and snatched away the bills with the other. It was all done so quickly that none of the men at the bar knew what had happened, and Allen was left speechless, his empty fingers clawing at the air.

Then Abe entered the picture. In three long strides he reached the sailor, who was just edging toward the door. The man's back was toward him. Abe caught him by the shoulder with iron fingers and jerked him around. And almost in the same motion he drove a solid smash to the fellow's chin with his right fist.

The sailor lost his balance, staggered back a step or two, and toppled to the floor. Quick as a flash Abe was on top of him, gripping his wrists in those big, horny paws of his. With an anguished groan the German let go of the roll of money, and Abe, picking it up, jumped to his feet. As he did so an empty bottle whizzed past his head, and half a dozen sailormen charged toward him from all parts of the room. Instantly pandemonium was let loose. With wild yells of delight the river-men, always ready for a fight, set upon the deep-water sailors, and in ten seconds the place was filled with fiercely struggling groups.

Abe stuffed the bills into the breast of his shirt and battled his way toward the door, where Tad was already waiting for him. In a moment Allen broke through the mob in front of the bar and joined them. His "store clothes" were disheveled, and one eye was nearly closed by a rapidly swelling bruise.

"Run—run!" he panted, and dodged down an alley with the two others following him. Not until they had zigzagged through the dark for two blocks and were out on the open levee front did Allen settle down once more to a walk.

"Great shiverin' snakes!" he gasped, "I was glad to git clear o' that place! Did ye see 'em start to pull their knives? Why, thar was enough dirks an' daggers out to slaughter a regiment.''

Silently Abe handed the crumpled banknotes back to their owner. A few steps farther he stopped. ''You boys wait here,'' he said. ''I forgot somethin', but I'll be right back.''

Dumfounded, they watched him stride along the levee in the direction from which they had just come.

''Whar in Sam Hill kin he be goin'?'' muttered Allen. They waited with growing nervousness for several minutes. And just as Tad was starting to see what had happened, he reappeared.

''Where were you, Abe?'' the boy asked.

''I'd clean forgot to pay fer our supper,'' Abe replied. ''Things had quieted down thar a mite, but one pore feller was bleedin' terrible. Cut pretty bad, I guess.''

''Wal,'' said Allen, looking at him, pop-eyed, ''if you ain't the gol-durnedest!''

''How'd you come to have all that money?'' inquired Abe. ''Must have sold the cargo, didn't ye?''

Allen nodded. ''A man come along the levee this afternoon offerin' scandalous low prices fer flour an' pork. I was gittin' sick o' waitin'; so I dickered with him. I got him to raise his figger a little, an' he 'greed to take the boat, too. Anyhow, Father'll be satisfied."

"He won't if you go in any more saloons an' git it stole," said Abe. "I reckon on board a steamboat is the safest place fer you an' me."

They returned to the *Katy Roby,* now empty save for their blankets and personal belongings, a few cooking utensils, and a small pile of firewood.

"The old gal looks sort o' lonesome, don't she?" said Abe. "Wal, her timbers'll make a stout shanty fer somebody. There's not a cross-grained stick in her hull. I know, because I cut an' trimmed 'em myself."

The other two were silent, for they also felt a twinge of homesickness at the idea of leaving the craft. Tad stretched out on the bare planking, ready for sleep after his miles of barefoot exploration. Soon he dropped off, in spite of the raucous chorus of drunken river-men returning to their boats, and it was to bright morning sunlight that he next opened his eyes. Abe was busy preparing some odds and ends of food for breakfast, while Allen sat back and plucked at his banjo strings. It was the old tune of "Skip to my Lou" that he was singing, but he had invented some new verses. Two of them were:

"'N'Orleans gals, you're feelin' blue,
N'Orleans gals, you're feelin' blue,
N'Orleans gals, you're feelin' blue,
Skip to my Lou, my darlin'.

"'We're bound to say good-by to you,
We're bound to say good-by to you,
We're bound to say good-by to you,
Skip to my Lou, my darlin'.''

He rolled his eyes sentimentally as he sang, and Abe chuckled over the frying-pan. "Wait till he gits back to Gentryville!" he said. "Folks up thar will git the idee that the whole valley's littered up with the hearts he's broke."

When breakfast was finished, Abe rolled up his ax and one or two other things he owned in his blanket, tied it with a rope, and laid it to one side.

"Now, Tad," said he, "we'll go an' rouse out this man McCann, so he kin tell that lunkhead in your father's office who you are."

They took their way along the levee in the direction of the steamboat landings. When they had covered a little over half the distance, they saw a two-horse carriage coming rapidly toward them, and as it drew close, Abe pulled Tad out of its path behind a pile of baled cotton. Thus it was not until the carriage had gone past that the boy had a good look at its occupant. He was a big-framed man of middle age, in a beaver hat that looked travel-stained. His head and shoulders were bowed slightly as if by a burden.

Tad seized Abe's arm. "That was my Dad!" he said. "He's on his way to the office from the boat. Come on!"

Quickly they turned and followed the carriage toward the older section of the town. A few minutes of alternate running and walking brought them to St. Louis Street, and at the curb, sure enough, they saw the carriage drawn up.

They went into the building and up the stairs, two at a time. The door of the office stood ajar. Tad entered first. There at his desk on the other side of the room sat his father, looking so gray and sad and careworn that Tad felt a great lump in his throat at the sight. He tried to shout "Dad!" but all that came was a choking sound.

The officious young secretary advanced from his corner with what was intended for a threatening scowl, but Tad paid no attention to him. Then Jeremiah Hopkins must have sensed that something was happening, for he looked up wearily from the papers in his hands and saw a boy at the gate—a ragged, barefoot youngster, brown as an

Indian, with a mop of sandy hair and a mouth that grinned broadly while his eyes blinked back something suspiciously like tears.

"D-don't you know me, Dad?" said the boy. And then Jeremiah Hopkins ran toward him and they caught each other in a bear-like hug.

The father's heart was too full for words, but he held the lad at arm's length and looked at him as if he could never get enough of the sight.

Tad's power of speech came back to him first, and he talked in happy, jumbled sentences, trying to tell everything at once.

"I wrote to you, Dad," he said, "but, you see, you never got my letter because it was blown up. It was on the *Nancy Jones*. But it's too bad you worried so about me. I was all right. Abe, here, was taking care of me, and— Come, I want you to meet him. Abe—"

But the young husky from Indiana was gone. He had slipped out quietly as soon as he saw his friend safe in his father's arms.

Tad ran down the stairs and looked up and down the street, but the lanky figure was nowhere in sight. Distressed, he returned to his father. "We must find him," he said. "You've got to know Abe, because he's the best friend I ever had. Why, he saved my life!"

The young secretary, very crestfallen, came forward. ''I—I think he went toward the levee, sir,'' said he.

''You should have asked him to wait,'' the merchant answered curtly. ''We'll go in search of him directly, Tad, my boy. But first come and get some clothes on.''

They got into the carriage and were driven, despite the boy's protestations, to Mr. Hopkins' hotel, where the clothes found in the stateroom on the steamboat had been taken. In a few minutes Tad was dressed once more in the garb of civilization.

''Now,'' said he, ''tell the coachman we want to go to the flatboat moorings as fast as he can drive.''

Through the streets and along the levee they rumbled and drew up at last where Tad pointed to the *Katy Roby,* tied up in the middle of the swarming river-craft. But Abe and Allen were nowhere to be seen.

The stout Kentucky man sat on the rail of his boat, near the levee, and spat judicially into the river before he answered Tad's eager query.

''No,'' said he, finally. ''They ain't here. They done picked up their blankets an' stuff an' put out fer the steamboat landin' some while back. Said they was goin' to go on the *Ohio Belle* if they got thar 'fore she sailed.''

Hurriedly the Hopkinses, father and son, climbed back into the carriage, and the coachman used his whip as they galloped toward the smoky forest of steamboat stacks.

''She's not gone yet,'' cried Tad. ''I can see her.''

But just then there came a long, deep whistle-blast, and one of the great white steamers began to move slowly away from the levee side. The carriage rolled up to the landing, and the coachman pulled the rearing horses to a stop. As Tad jumped out he saw a tall, awkward youth in homespun and deerskin waving to him from the forward rail of the upper deck.

''Abe,'' he cried, ''wait! wait!''

''Come back!'' shouted his father, ''I want to give you the reward.'' And he held up a fat black wallet.

One of Abe's quaint grins overspread his homely face. ''No,'' he called back. ''He was a good hand an' earned his keep.''

Tad ran forward to the edge of the levee and cupped his hands about his mouth. ''Abe,'' he yelled, ''what's your last name? I want to write to you.''

"Lincoln," the backwoods boy replied. "Jest send it to Gentryville. They'll see that I git it."

Then with a clang of bells and a great splashing of foam as her paddles beat the water, the *Ohio Belle* swung out into the current and headed upstream. And the last thing Tad saw was Abe picking up the little bear, Poke, in his arms, and waving one of the cub's black paws in a comical good-by.